FOREVER C

The Gilbert G

by Cat Cahill

Chapter One

Crest Stone, Colorado Territory, 1875

If she remained perfectly still and quiet, perhaps the conductor would look past her. She could stay on this train forever and ever, traveling for eternity from Denver to Santa Fe and back again, just as much a fixture in this car as the seats or the doors.

"Miss? Miss, are you all right? Isn't this your stop?" The conductor stared down at her, concern drawing his features into lines.

"I—I'm fine." Elizabeth Campbell forced her legs to stand.

The conductor took a step back, but still didn't look convinced that Elizabeth could make it from the seat to the door without swooning or some such nonsense. "Do you need assistance?"

"No, I don't. I was merely asleep." She brushed past him, speaking more harshly than she'd intended, but her nerves were making her feel as if everything was rushed. Her heart beat in triple time, her stomach ached, and if her hands weren't clenched around the handles of a carpetbag, she knew her fingers would be trembling.

Elizabeth took the hand of another conductor and stepped down onto the small platform. She was in no hurry, despite what her heart might think. She wouldn't be reboarding the train—at least not today.

She blinked into the bright noon sun that glittered off the snow but did nothing to warm the air. It would be so easy to turn around, go right back up those steps, and become part of the seat again. No one expected her. No one knew where she was.

And no one particularly cared.

Pinching her lower lip between her teeth, Elizabeth forced away thoughts of the life she'd left behind in California. The past was the past. She was free now, and that's what she needed to keep in mind. All she needed to do was enter that hotel, inquire after her brother, and hope he was happy to see her.

"Carriage, miss?" A driver, dressed in a neat black coat, smiled and held out a hand to take her bag.

Elizabeth glanced between him and the hotel. It would be a frosty walk up the snow-covered hill to reach her destination. But as much as she relished the idea of a ride, she didn't have so much as a penny left to give the man for a tip. "No, but thank you. I'm looking forward to the exercise."

The man touched his hat as Elizabeth smiled at him. She stepped off the wooden planks outside the depot and into the snow that had been pressed down from the carriage wheels. It was best to get it over with. That seemed like the sort of advice her mother might've given her, if she'd lived long enough.

By the time she reached the grand hotel doors, Elizabeth was thankful for her coat and boots, as threadbare as they were. A bellhop opened the door and attempted to reach for her bag. Elizabeth pulled it to her with a smile as she stepped inside. It took a moment for her eyes to adjust, but when they did, she nearly gasped.

The wooden desk and floors gleamed, beams stretched across the tall ceiling, flames roared in the giant stone fireplaces on either end of the enormous lobby, stairs gracefully led the way to the upper floor, and finely clothed men and women bustled about. The only things missing were Yuletide decorations. Crest Stone might not have been much of a town at all, but this hotel was as fine as any establishment she would've been too afraid to step into in Denver. She didn't dare remove her coat, or else everyone would be able to tell she didn't belong in such a place.

A friendly-looking girl with shining blonde hair, a perfectly starched gray dress, and an apron that would have been white if it wasn't for an unsightly coffee stain, stopped in front of her. "Good afternoon, miss. Are you in search of the dining room? Or perhaps the lunch counter? It isn't as nice, but the soup is hot and filling."

Elizabeth forced herself to smile through the wave of fear that rolled through her yet again. "I'm . . . I'm to meet someone. My brother." It was only the tiniest of lies, considering he had no idea she was here.

"Oh? What is his name? I might be able to point you in his direction if he's staying here."

"Monroe Hartley. I've been told he built this hotel."

The girl tilted her head, clearly confused. "I don't believe he's still in residence here."

Elizabeth nearly dropped her carpetbag. "What do you mean?" she asked, her voice barely a whisper. Of all the outcomes she'd contemplated, this wasn't one of them.

"Maybe he's planning to return and hasn't arrived yet?" the girl said.

"No," Elizabeth said, her fingers gripping the handle of her bag. "I . . . I must be mistaken. I'm sorry to have troubled you. I'll . . ." She glanced about the room. Where would she go? Even if Monroe turned her away, she'd assumed he would've given her the fare to at least return to Denver.

"I'm so sorry to have disappointed you. Do you need a room for the night? I can take you to the front desk."

"No, I can't—" Elizabeth's voice rose and cracked on the last word. She wouldn't cry. She hadn't cried in years, and she didn't intend to start now. "It's only . . . I don't know . . ."

"You must sit." The girl took her hand and led her to a large wing chair that flanked the nearby fireplace. "I'm Adelaide. I work here, as a waitress. Do you need something to drink? Would that help?"

Elizabeth shook her head as she set her bag down. Nothing would help. Not now. Why had she been so foolish when she was younger? Everything could have turned out so much better for her if she'd just listened to her brother and to Colette. But she hadn't, and now here she was—widowed, penniless, and entirely alone. "I have nowhere to go," she finally said, her words strangled.

Adelaide knelt beside her and patted her hand. "I know just the thing. Stay right here." And with that, she was up and weaving through the chairs and people toward the hallway beyond the stairs.

Elizabeth barely had time to contemplate what Adelaide was doing when the girl returned, a kindly-looking woman trailing behind her.

"This is Mrs. McFarland," Adelaide said to Elizabeth. "She helps run the hotel. Mrs. McFarland, this is—oh, goodness. I didn't ask your name. My mother would positively die. Please forgive me."

Elizabeth almost laughed despite her predicament. She stood and forced her voice to remain steady. "Mrs. Campbell. Elizabeth."

"It's a pleasure to meet you, dear." Mrs. McFarland clasped Elizabeth's hand between her own, and her smile warmed Elizabeth to her bones. She had the strangest feeling this woman wouldn't care about any of the mistakes Elizabeth had made in the past. "Now, Adelaide here tells me you're in some distress?"

Elizabeth chewed on her lip for a moment while she thought about what to say. Adelaide spoke first. "She came to meet her brother, Mr.—"

"It's quite all right," Elizabeth said quickly, cutting off her maiden name from Adelaide's tongue. There was no need to embarrass herself—or her brother—any further. He wasn't here, and Elizabeth preferred to keep his potential disappointment in her to herself. She gathered herself, standing a little taller and placing her hands against her stomach for strength. There was nothing to be ashamed of in what had happened to her recently, after all. "I've found myself stranded. My husband died suddenly at a mining camp in California. I came here to meet family, but it appears they've moved on. I'm without means to search for them any further, or to return . . . anywhere." She glanced at Adelaide. The girl gave her an encouraging smile, and an idea struck Elizabeth.

"Perhaps I could work here? Only for a while, until I've saved enough for train fare and until I've located my family. If you're in need, that is."

Mrs. McFarland opened her mouth to speak, but Elizabeth pressed on. "I'm quite capable. I can sweep, cook, do laundry. Anything you might need." She didn't add that she'd never worked for pay. Colin had forbidden it, even when they'd not had a cent to buy a tin of beans.

"Mrs. Campbell, you seem well-spoken and mannered. May I ask your background?" Mrs. McFarland said.

Elizabeth wanted to sink into the chair in relief. Mrs. McFarland must be considering her request, or else she wouldn't ask such a thing. "My family came from Kansas City originally, but I grew up in Denver. My mother died when I was young, and my father when I was fifteen. We didn't have much, but I never wanted for anything. And my brother always looked out for me. I married young and went to California with my husband. He was a ranch hand who then became a miner. It was hard. He was . . ." She pushed past those memories. "I did my best to stay away from the more unsavory aspects of the camp. I kept house and went to services as often as I could."

Mrs. McFarland clasped her hands together, her eyes still on Elizabeth. She radiated nothing but kindness, but Elizabeth wanted to squirm. She'd told the truth, even if she had glossed over many of the more unpleasant aspects of her life—including what she'd done to her brother.

"Would you be interested in a position as one of our Gilbert Girls?" Mrs. McFarland finally asked.

Adelaide must have noticed Elizabeth's confusion, because she added, "A waitress."

"Yes," Elizabeth said. "Yes, of course. Are you certain?"

"We'll give it a try," the woman replied. "We'll see how you do for a few weeks. If at that point, you'd like to collect your wages and leave, you may. Or if it goes well and you'd like to stay, you'd be able to sign a contract for a year."

It was more than Elizabeth could have hoped for. A waitress was a far more respectable position than a maid. And it likely paid more too. "That sounds wonderful. Thank you very much."

"You're welcome, my dear. We needed to replace a girl who is getting married. You arrived at just the right time. I must tell you, though, you're the first girl we've hired on the premises. Most of the others go through rigorous interviews back East before traveling out here, but I have a good feeling about you." She smiled at Elizabeth before turning to the younger girl. "Adelaide, will you take Mrs. Campbell upstairs? She can stay with Sarah. I'll send one of the maids up with some dresses and linens."

Adelaide nodded, and before Elizabeth could truly fathom what had just happened, she was whisked up the polished wood stairs to the second floor to begin a new life.

Chapter Two

Landon Cooper didn't need a hotel. He didn't need a meal. And he certainly didn't need to stop riding. Yet somehow, he found himself leading his horse to the stables at the Crest Stone Hotel and Restaurant and nearly salivating at the thought of hot food that didn't taste like salt pork or stale bread.

A night here wouldn't hurt anything, after all. He wasn't due in Cañon City for several days. A real bed and a fire to warm his hands might even remind him he was making the right decision. He could barely think straight on horseback in this weather, and it led to all kinds of doubts he had no business entertaining.

Inside, he found the fire he'd been craving. The massive fireplace thawed his frozen hands almost instantly, and his fingers tingled as the blood began pumping through them again. Landon would've been perfectly happy to slump into one of the fireplace chairs for the night, but his stomach wouldn't quit reminding him that he needed food.

Merry laughter and the sound of forks tinkling against china plates came from a large dining room nearby. Landon took a couple of steps in that direction, his mouth almost watering at the scent of what had to be beef stew.

"Sir?" An uppity male voice made him halt.

Landon turned to find a man leaning over the front desk. "Yes?"

"Sir," the man said again, his eyes taking in Landon's worn and dirty coat, boots wet from the snow, and trousers that had run into one too many filthy cattle. "Might I suggest you'd be more comfortable at our lunch counter?"

"Might I suggest you keep your suggestions to yourself?"

The man's pinched face drooped, and he looked down, busying himself with some papers lying on the desk.

Landon was almost disappointed. But what did he expect—for this pasty fellow from somewhere back East to leap over the desk and fight him? He was restless, and that made him easily agitated, and *that* made it far too easy for him to begin looking for trouble. He shook his head to clear it. Maybe he really did need a few days to think through all of this. If he could feel completely certain of his decision, that restless feeling might go away.

He headed toward the door with the sign that indicated it housed the lunch counter—but only because he wanted to, not because anyone said he should.

A long, oval-shaped counter took up most of the small room. In the middle, two pretty girls in gray and white chatted with customers and refilled mugs of steaming coffee. Landon could almost taste the coffee just from the scent of it. The customers looked rough—all men and most of them appearing as if they hadn't had a bath or changed clothes in months. Landon glanced down at his own clothing and winced. He certainly fit in here.

He took a free seat far away from the others. If he sat too close to anyone, they'd want to engage in conversation. And conversation was the last thing Landon needed at the moment. One of the waitresses brought him a cup of coffee, and he cradled it between his hands like a newborn calf. The heat seemed to melt into his bones, and—for a moment—his irritation with everything settled into a corner of his mind.

If only he could sit here with a hot cup of coffee for the rest of the winter. Come spring, he could get hired on again at one of the nearby ranches, as he'd done since he was sixteen.

Landon frowned into his mug. It would be the same thing, every year, until he'd finally saved up enough money to start his own place. He could get a piece of land for cheap if he agreed to homestead it for five years, but a piece of land with no house or cattle or men to work it wouldn't be much of a ranch. And he'd be an old man before he could afford that, too old to really enjoy it, and too old to work alongside men he would hire. No, something had to change. He only wished he had an option other than the one waiting for him in Cañon City.

He tapped a boot against the foot rail and searched the counter for one of the waitresses. Real food would help him think straight, help him fully commit to what he needed to do.

A third waitress appeared behind the counter from the little door on the opposite side. This one seemed distracted. She fumbled with the strings of her apron and then tripped over something Landon couldn't see on the floor.

"Miss?" he finally called, seeing as she was the one nearest him.

She twisted to see behind her as she messed with those apron strings again.

"Miss?" Landon said, a little louder this time. "Could I get something to eat?"

She finally lifted her head, a pair of dark eyes surrounded by an angelic face and light brown hair swept up behind her waitress's hat. She said something, but he didn't hear.

He couldn't do anything but stare.

Chapter Three

E lizabeth had met Mrs. Ruby, the dining-room manager, who insisted she be properly trained before being allowed to serve guests in the dining room. And so Elizabeth found herself at the lunch counter. She was supposed to emulate the other two girls. Mrs. Ruby had made it sound simple, and yet Elizabeth already felt as if she were intended to do anything *but* this.

Now this man was staring as if something were wrong with her. Elizabeth glanced down at her clothing, but all seemed to be in place—even those pesky apron strings were finally tied. She casually ran a hand across her face and then smiled at the man, hoping he'd finally speak. He certainly was handsome enough, with striking eyes and a strong jaw, even if it did look as though he'd slept in those clothes.

"Sir?" she said again, twisting her hands together. She was growing warm under the gaze of those blue eyes. They weren't an average sort of blue either; they were darker, like the deepest part of a mountain lake. "What is it you'd like to eat?"

He blinked, finally, and his Adam's apple bobbed as he seemed to become aware of the rest of the room. "Have you got any of the beef stew that's in the dining room?"

Elizabeth had no idea if they did or not. But she didn't care. She'd go to the dining room herself and fetch him a bowl of soup if she had to. "Yes. I could get that for you."

He nodded. There was no "thank you" or "that would be good" or any other sort of friendly nicety. Elizabeth could've laughed at herself. Here she was, willing to wait hand and foot on a man who was no better than her former husband. Colin had also had that way of looking at her as if she were the only person in the world, and she'd foolishly followed him anywhere he wanted to go. Judging from this man's clothing and his lack of manners, he was also a cowboy.

9

Elizabeth had learned her lesson about cowboys.

"What I meant," she amended, "is that I must ask one of the other girls. This is my first day here, and I'm not certain what we have."

"All right," the man said, his words a little clipped. She'd annoyed him, and part of her felt good about that. Yet she felt those eyes on her even as she walked to the far end of the counter.

She found one of the other waitresses, a petite girl with dark blonde curls bursting from her chignon, and asked her about the stew.

"You must be the new girl! I'm Genia. And yes, we can get the beef stew. We can get anything they have in the dining room, plus any soups the chef has made or any food left over from lunch. We take turns running orders back to the kitchen. I'll take yours since I've already got a couple of my own."

"Thank you," Elizabeth said, grateful for the help. She didn't even know who to talk to in the kitchen. She'd have to ask Genia later. For now, she returned to the cowboy, who was watching her with neither a smile nor a frown. Elizabeth wasn't certain what to make of that. Was he happy or upset? It didn't matter much to her, except that she didn't want an unhappy customer on her first day. "I can get your stew."

That should have made him smile, but his expression remained impassive. "Thank you," he finally said.

So he wasn't entirely devoid of manners. Elizabeth glanced around the counter. The other customers appeared tended to. She supposed she was now required to make conversation with her customers. And seeing as this cowboy was her only one, she drew a deep breath and plunged in. "Are you staying at the hotel?"

"I am," he said slowly as he leaned back in his chair.

Elizabeth clasped her hands together. Talking to this man was exasperating. And yet she felt compelled to know more about him. "Where are you headed?"

"Why do you want to know?"

She bit back a sharp reply. Experience had taught her that nothing good ever came from a retort. "I'm simply making conversation."

He narrowed those lake-colored eyes. "Cañon City," he finally said.

"Oh." Elizabeth was at a loss for what to say next. She knew nothing about Cañon City aside from what she'd seen through the train window. And conversing was quite difficult when only one person made the effort. But Mrs. Ruby and Mrs. McFarland were depending on her. And unless she wanted to wash bedding and scrub floors, she needed to try harder to succeed at this job. "Are you going there for Christmas?"

"Christmas?" The man said the word as if he'd never heard it before.

"Yes," Elizabeth said slowly. "Do you have family there for the holidays?"

"No."

Elizabeth bit down on her lip. This was ridiculous. Where was that stew? Surely no one expected her to stand here and talk to this man as he ate. She forged ahead. "I adore Christmas. I especially love hanging boughs of pine and ribbons and cooking the Christmas meal. Even the saddest accommodations can look cheerful with a little decorating." Her smile this time was genuine. Colin had never much noticed her efforts at Christmas, but the act of making their tiny shack festive had always lightened Elizabeth's mood, even in the darkest of times.

The cowboy was staring at her again. She ran her hands over her apron and prayed harder than she'd ever prayed before that the stew would arrive. "What is your business in Cañon City then, if not to visit family?"

His expressionless face finally cracked, but not in the way Elizabeth hoped. He frowned, and that stare turned into a glare. "Work."

"It doesn't seem like something you're much looking forward to," she said lightly. She winced at her tone. It was the same one she'd taken time and again with Colin. The one she used when she tried to turn his anger into something else—anything else.

But the cowboy didn't grow angry. Instead, he ran a hand through his dark hair and said, "You're right. It isn't."

"Then you should find something else to do instead," she said.

The little bit of life she'd been able to pull from him disappeared again into a sullen frown, and he said nothing at all.

"Miss?" An older man had joined the counter a few seats down. But Elizabeth couldn't pull her eyes off the customer she already had. What was it that weighed so heavily on this man's shoulders?

And why did she care?

"You have another customer," he said, not looking at her at all now.

Elizabeth had to ask the older man to repeat his order several times before she could remember it. Genia returned with the blue-eyed cowboy's beef stew as Elizabeth made her way to the kitchen to attempt to place orders. When she returned, the man was gone.

She was strangely disappointed. And then instantly frustrated with herself. The last thing she needed in her life right now was another cowboy.

Chapter Four

Landon exited the lunch counter room feeling as if he'd drunk a bottle of whiskey when in fact he hadn't touched the stuff in years. The stew and the coffee had done him a world of good, but that woman . . . She threw all of his senses into a whirl. It was impossible for anyone to look as if they'd come straight down from heaven, and yet, there she was.

The way she kept talking to him, it was as if she didn't care one whit that he made it clear he didn't wish to converse. And yet, as she went on and on about Christmas, he almost didn't want her to stop. Her voice was like music, soft and lyrical. Without even knowing him, she said the one thing that had gotten right to the heart of his unease.

Why couldn't he do something else?

The answer was easy: there *was* nothing else. Not for him, anyway. And not if he wanted to change his situation fast. Of course, she wouldn't understand that. With that angel face and those big, innocent eyes, she'd never believe him if he told her.

Finally feeling as if his feet would carry him to the front desk, Landon made his way there and requested a room from the pompous clerk. The man's expression changed considerably when Landon withdrew the cash from his pocket. It was money he shouldn't be spending, not if he intended to build up a spread of his own one day, and yet if he spent one more night out in the cold, he'd lose his mind completely.

Landon's room was on the second floor, tucked back and away at the end of the hallway that stretched the length of the hotel's south wing. It was comfortably appointed and filled with touches he imagined wealthy guests might appreciate. As for Landon, all that concerned him was the comfort of the bed and the warmth of the room.

But even after he lay down, worn out from riding, he found himself staring at the ceiling and imagining a pretty, golden brown-haired waitress telling him how important it was to hang stockings from the mantel. He smiled at the image. He'd never even asked her name.

And that was for the best. Frustrated, he turned over and forced himself to imagine what her expression might be if he told her why he was going to Cañon City.

That pretty pink mouth would frown and her eyes would narrow in judgment. Then she'd never speak to him again, which was just as well. He was better off on his own. Even if his reasoning was sound, it didn't excuse the method by which he planned to get what he wanted. No woman deserved to be with a man like him. Aimee had ensured he understood that well enough last year.

And she was right. He was too frustrated all the time. Too prone to acting on a whim. Devoid of any social graces. Nothing but a poor, filthy ranch hand. And by next week, when that angel downstairs was baking a Christmas pie and singing carols, he'd be an outlaw.

Chapter Five

"I've determined we need no less than eight different pies," Penny, the tall girl with brown curls, said as she set down the napkin she was supposed to be teaching Elizabeth to fold.

"Eight?" Dora, the quieter girl with the dark hair, deftly folded her napkin before glancing up at her friend.

Elizabeth concentrated on folding while the two girls Mrs. Ruby had asked to train her discussed their upcoming weddings.

"Yes. Apple, pumpkin, cherry—" Penny counted them off on her fingers.

"Where do you expect to find cherries this time of year?" Dora asked.

"Chef Pourrin can find all sorts of food." Penny waved her hand in the general direction of the kitchen.

"I think we should let Mrs. Ruby decide. After all, she's being kind enough to let us use the dining room for our wedding luncheon." Dora glanced up at Elizabeth and gave her a tiny, conspiratorial smile.

Elizabeth bit her lip to keep from smiling too. Dora seemed to have a way with taming Penny's wilder ideas. Elizabeth marveled at how close the two of them seemed to be, especially considering the hotel had only been open a few months. She held up her own napkin folded into the shape of a flower.

"You're good at that," Penny said. "You'll make a finer Gilbert Girl than I ever was."

Given how much she'd struggled at the lunch counter the day before, Elizabeth wasn't so certain. But folding napkins was a thousand times easier than making conversation with reticent customers. Perhaps if she did at least some things well enough, Mrs. Ruby might overlook her faults when it came to serving guests.

"Aren't you still working? I mean, since you aren't married yet?" Elizabeth asked, wishing she could take back the question as soon as it was out of her mouth. As curious as she was, it was far too intrusive to ask someone she'd only just met.

Penny and Dora glanced at each other and smiled, and Elizabeth had the distinct impression she'd missed out on something very entertaining.

"Didn't Mrs. McFarland or Mrs. Ruby go over the rules with you yet?" Dora asked gently.

Elizabeth shook her head. She hadn't even seen Mrs. McFarland since yesterday, and she'd only spoken with Mrs. Ruby in passing.

"Gilbert Girls are not allowed to be courted while under contract with the company," Penny said in a nasal voice. She grinned at her friend. "Dora and I weren't so good at following the rules."

Dora's cheeks reddened. "We aren't the first."

"I doubt we'll be the last. It's too difficult with all these handsome men coming in and out of this hotel. You'll see, Elizabeth. You'll have all good intentions to remain true to your word, and then out of nowhere, some tall, dark-haired cowboy comes riding up and sweeps you off your feet." Penny sighed.

"Sheriff Young isn't dark-haired or a cowboy," Dora said.

"Silly, I didn't mean him. I was imagining the perfect man for Elizabeth." Penny grinned at Elizabeth, completely unaware that she'd just about described the man at the lunch counter yesterday.

Elizabeth dug for words, needing desperately to divert her thoughts from the man with the eyes she was certain she'd never forget, despite his abrupt manner. "What do you mean, you aren't the first? Hasn't this hotel only been open for a few months?"

"Our dear friend Caroline married Mr. Drexel—in jail, no less!—in October. They run the general store now. But before them, Emma married Mr. Hartley," Penny said as she folded her napkin.

"Mr. Hartley?" Elizabeth could barely get her own maiden name out. It was the first she'd heard of her brother since Adelaide had told her he was no longer at the hotel. Monroe was married, and not to Colette. Elizabeth's mind spun. What had happened to Colette?

"He built the hotel," Dora said. "He went all the way to Kentucky to win Emma back after she thought he didn't care for her."

"It was so very romantic." Penny tossed her half-folded napkin aside.

"Did they remain there?" Elizabeth tried to keep her fingers busy and her eyes on her hands so as not to give anything away. She should have written Monroe. She always meant to, when she and Colin had settled in to their new lives in California, but it never seemed the right time. Especially when her married life turned out not to be the dream she'd imagined when they'd left.

"Oh, no," Dora said. "They returned here, separately—"

"That's a story," Penny interrupted.

"After they married and rebuilt the hotel, Monroe took work in California," Dora finished.

"But they're due back here any day!" Penny grinned. "Just in time to see us get married."

"They're coming back?" Elizabeth repeated. She was still digesting the fact that he'd arrived in California only a few months before she'd left. Perhaps she wouldn't have to chase Monroe down to the ends of the earth. According to Dora and Penny, it wouldn't be that much longer until he'd have the opportunity to tell her how horrible and selfish she was and send her packing off to who even knew where. He'd likely tell her she deserved what she'd gotten in California after being so ungrateful to him.

Or maybe he wouldn't. But Elizabeth almost didn't dare hope.

"Yes. They should arrive any day now," Dora said. She surveyed the napkins they'd folded. "Perhaps we should move on to etiquette."

As Dora spoke of properly greeting guests and the art of figuring out whether a customer wanted conversation or preferred to be left alone, Elizabeth's mind drifted back to that cowboy yesterday. She knew now, with what Dora said, that she shouldn't have pressed him to talk with her. Attempting to converse with him was like washing out an impossible stain. She should've left well enough alone once it was clear he was in no mood to speak. She wondered what his manner was like when he didn't have something so heavy sitting on his mind. He likely wasn't much different, but maybe he was less sharp and prone to jumping to conclusions.

Elizabeth sighed. She'd be wise to stay away from this man. He was a cowboy, and they were all the same, even when they entered a new line of work. If she ever married again, it would be to a staid man with a dull sort of a job. A bookkeeper, perhaps, or a salesman.

"Elizabeth?" Dora said gently.

"Yes?" Elizabeth blinked away her wandering thoughts. Dora and Penny were standing, and Elizabeth supposed her waitress training was over for now.

"Did you hear me? We were hoping you might like to help us decorate the hotel for Christmas."

"That would be wonderful! I adore decorating." Elizabeth couldn't keep the smile from her face. "Where should we start? I have some time before Mrs. Ruby expects me to work."

Penny laughed. "We were thinking this evening, but why not begin now?"

"Do we have ribbon? Bows on the pine boughs would be lovely, don't you think? We'll need to gather those, of course. Are there any red berries that grow here? Should we ask about getting a tree? I haven't had a tree since I was child." Ideas flowed faster than Elizabeth could put them into words.

As she looped arms with Penny and Dora, she realized she felt different than she had in a long time.

She was happy.

Chapter Six

Outside was the last place Landon wanted to be, but his horse wouldn't check on himself. He needn't have bothered, however. The hotel's stable hands had already given Ulysses breakfast and had turned him out in the corral.

Now he stood, halfway between the stables and the hotel with a very light snow drifting down, wondering if it would be such a terrible thing if he stayed here one more night. It would be less expensive if he moved on to Cañon City, where he could get a room for a fraction of the cost of this hotel, and cost was important to a man who saved nearly every dime he earned. But he'd also need to meet up with Redmond and the others once he was there. He needed to be certain he wanted to go through with this job when he did that.

And as much as he hated to admit it, he wasn't. Not yet.

He let out a frustrated sigh. Landon had never been one to be indecisive, until now. Aimee had made it clear that no one thought he was any sort of upstanding gentleman, so why did taking his future into his own hands this way bother him so much? What Redmond had planned wouldn't hurt anyone. It was simply sharing the wealth, and Landon desperately needed some of that wealth if he wanted his own ranch before he was eighty. He'd certainly worked hard enough for it over the years.

He fisted and unfisted his hands, trying to keep them from freezing. He should get back to the hotel and take advantage of the warmth that waited inside. Just as he took a step forward, movement off to the left, at a line of trees that flanked Silver Creek, caught Landon's eye. He squinted through the slowly drifting flurries. The figure was a woman, and she was struggling with . . . something.

He couldn't tell if it was a person or an animal, but she clearly needed help. Trudging through the snow on a rescue mission was not at all what he had in mind, particularly when those fireplaces inside beckoned him, but he wasn't one to leave a woman in distress on her own.

Landon moved faster toward the trees. Even as he grew closer, he couldn't tell what awaited him. He'd left his guns inside, and he hoped that whatever it was, it could be easily dispelled without needing a weapon.

He drew up a few feet away in disbelief. This woman wasn't in any danger, unless the tree branches came to life and began attacking. She seemed to be doing a good enough number on the boughs already—they wouldn't have stood a chance.

"Ma'am?" he said, removing his hat. "Might I ask if you need any help?" He was already here, so he might as well offer.

She turned abruptly, pressing a hand to her heart. "You startled me." Familiar brown eyes looked back at him. If it was possible for this woman to look even more like an angel, she'd accomplished it. A worn hood covered her hair, but her eyes sparkled and her skin looked softer than the snow beneath Landon's feet. "It's you," she said, her face reddening as soon as the words were out of her mouth. "I'm sorry, I don't know your name."

"Landon Cooper." He tried to keep his eyes off the attractive blush that still colored her cheeks, but it was impossible. The color only deepened as he held her gaze, and something about that pleased him.

"I am Elizabeth Campbell," she finally said in a slightly strained voice. "And I'm attempting to cut those branches to use as decoration in the hotel." She held up a small saw. "But I fear I'm useless with this."

Landon replaced his hat and held out his hand. She handed him the saw and stepped back. Cutting pine branches in the snow seemed useless and like a good way to freeze to death, but he wasn't about to let her continue fighting with that saw. He cut a couple of branches effortlessly. "How many of these do you need, Miss Campbell?"

"Mrs. Campbell," she corrected him.

He dropped the saw to his side as a strange sense of disappointment washed through him. "Are you married?" He wondered what sort of husband she had if she was required to work as a waitress. Not a very good one, clearly.

"I'm widowed." She looked past him to the tree, and he had the feeling she wished not to discuss the topic.

He nodded and turned back to the tree, a slight smile lifting the corners of his lips. He immediately forced it away. He might be well on his way to becoming an outlaw, but he didn't need to leave all manner of decency behind. Taking delight in a man's death was not only wrong, but shameful.

But it wasn't that, exactly, that had made him smile. He didn't know what it was. Thinking any further down that road would be a mistake. It was better that he let it be.

"How many of these do you need, Mrs. Campbell?" he asked again.

"Oh, I don't know. The hotel is awfully large. Fifty, maybe? A hundred seems too many."

"Fifty?" he repeated. "You'll scalp the trees bare. I'll cut you twenty."

"That won't be enough," she said, shifting the two he'd already cut in her arms. "I need some for all the doorways, the front desk, the fireplaces—"

"Twenty," he said. "For now."

Her face screwed up into a frown. An angry angel. He wanted to laugh, but pressed his lips together to keep from doing so and began sawing the next branch.

"Fine," she said from behind him. "I'll take twenty, but only if you agree to carry these inside for me."

"All right," he said before he realized what terms he'd accepted. Somehow, she'd gotten him to not only cut these ridiculous branches for her, but to also carry them inside like a pack mule. "If you find you need more, I'll cut them for you tomorrow," he then found himself saying.

She stood by quietly—for a change—as he cut the remaining boughs. Then he gathered them from her and they made their way back into the hotel.

"Thank you," she said as he placed the pile in front of one of the fireplaces.

"They'll need to dry before you can hang them." Landon shrugged off his coat and gloves. "Lest you want melting snow dripping on your guests."

Mrs. Campbell glanced at the branches. "I don't suppose I could request your help in one more thing?"

Landon sighed inwardly. "What would that be?"

She turned those big brown eyes on him and spoke in that musical voice. "I'd like to hang some of these over the dining-room doors. Would you be so kind to do that for me tomorrow, once they're dry?"

"Of course," he said immediately before he realized what he was committing himself to. "If I'm here. I may be leaving first thing in the morning." It was what he should do. He needed to get to Cañon City, and spending more time with this snow angel was not part of his plan. Even if he had already promised to cut more for her tomorrow.

"Oh, I see." Her voice dropped, and the disappointment was evident. "I'll ask one of the handymen. I didn't mean to bother you."

"It's no bother," he said gruffly. "If I'm here."

He needed to get out of there. Now. Before he agreed to hang the moon for her. He tugged on his hat, letting that serve as a goodbye, and turned abruptly to walk toward the lunch counter. It might be too early to eat the noon meal, but it was best to get it out of the way while Mrs. Campbell wasn't working.

There was nothing about him that deserved her attention. And it was best he stopped it now, before it grew to anything more.

Chapter Seven

The next morning, Elizabeth was up hours before the sun. She smiled as she washed her face and dressed, and then fairly skipped to the door. Her roommate, Sarah, who was the head waitress, was still fast asleep. But Elizabeth had work to do, and she couldn't stay in bed a moment longer.

Ideas for how to use the pine boughs and the ribbon Penny and Dora had purchased from the general store and mercantile had danced through her dreams all night. Some were ridiculous, as dreams often were, but some might prove to be useful. Mostly, she just couldn't wait to begin transforming the hotel into a place filled with holiday cheer. It would be the perfect setting for two Christmas day weddings.

Elizabeth flew down the stairs. The hotel was silent this early in the morning. The desk clerk, a Mr. Gilbert who Elizabeth had learned was Dora's intended, nodded at her as she passed. It seemed utterly unfair that he was allowed to keep his position here while Dora had to relinquish her role as a Gilbert Girl, but Elizabeth supposed this was an extraordinary case given that Mr. Gilbert's family owned the hotel. Dora had told her the entire story over supper in the kitchen last night. It sounded like something straight out of a dime novel, with a secret identity, a mystery, a thief, and a grave moment of peril, all winding up in Mr. Gilbert declaring his love for Dora as they saved the hotel. The whole thing was incredibly romantic, as Penny put it, and it made Elizabeth all the more eager to help make her new friends' weddings as perfect as possible.

The pine boughs rested where Mr. Cooper had left them yesterday in front of the fireplace near the dining-room doors. The lengths of red velvet ribbon the other girls had purchased lay nearby. She'd start with the mantels. In one of her dreams, she'd imagined the fireplaces blazing with flames as pine boughs, ribbon, and a candelabra festooned the mantels and stockings hung from each side. The stockings might be a bit much. This was a hotel, after all, and not a home with children. Perhaps the general store had something else festive she could add. For now, she'd just hang the branches and ribbon, and later she'd ask Mrs. Ruby if there were any spare candelabra.

Elizabeth had just put the finishing touches on the ribbon when she looked up and realized the breakfast service was well underway. Guests gathered throughout the lobby, and she noted with pride that some were admiring her work on the other fireplace. She'd always wanted a fireplace mantel to make festive. All they'd had at the camp in California was a persnickety woodstove, and that was no good for decorating. Not that Colin would have taken notice. She had to admit it felt nice to see people enjoying her efforts.

She stepped back to ensure the second mantel looked the way she wanted, and it was then she spotted Mr. Cooper making his way across the lobby toward the lunch counter. So he hadn't left after all, at least not yet.

Her heart beat harder as she approached him. "Mr. Cooper, you're just who I was hoping to see."

His face went ruddy beneath the dark stubble that dotted his cheeks and chin. "I don't have time to chop down any trees today, Mrs. Campbell," he said warily.

Elizabeth laughed. "No, I only wish to engage your efforts in hanging the pine boughs over the dining-room doors. After the breakfast service is completed, of course. Would you help me? Unless you need to be on your way, that is."

"I . . ." His eyes drifted to the hotel doors before landing back on her. He ran a hand through his hair and sighed. "I suppose I could."

"Oh, thank you!" Elizabeth gripped his hand, imagining how lovely the lobby would look once the doors were decorated. "I so appreciate your help. It will look marvelous when we're finished!"

He glanced down at her hands wrapped around his, and Elizabeth's face warmed. What had she done? Her enthusiasm had gotten the better of her good sense. She yanked her hands away and clasped them in front of her. "Thank you," she said again, more demurely this time. "I'll be here when you've finished your breakfast."

He nodded quickly and disappeared into the lunch counter room faster than a jackrabbit running from a hunter. Elizabeth stood, fixed to the floor. What had gotten into her? First, instead of telling him she was not allowed to be alone with him when he'd offered to cut those branches yesterday, she'd let him help her. And now she was grabbing him by the hand as if they'd been acquainted for years and years. He must think her quite ill-bred, if not downright devoid of any sense of morality.

She resolved to think before she acted or spoke from here on out. Her reputation and her position here depended upon it. She needed this work to afford train fare if Monroe never came. And if he did—and he decided she must leave—she'd at least have something to live on once she returned to Denver. It would do her no good at all to be acting so familiar with a man like Mr. Cooper.

When Mr. Cooper emerged from the lunch counter, Elizabeth had already eaten her own quick breakfast from the kitchen, decided which boughs needed to go over the dining-room doors, and had asked one of the bellboys to fetch a ladder, some nails, and a hammer.

Thankfully, Mr. Cooper said nothing about her familiarity earlier. In fact, he said nothing at all. Instead he set up the ladder as soon as Mrs. Ruby shut the dining-room doors, climbed up, and held out a hand.

Elizabeth stared at his hand. What did he want? Did he expect her to take it? She should've known better. Men who worked on ranches and drove cattle were all alike. And she hadn't helped at all with the way she'd acted earlier. If he thought she—

"A nail and hammer, if you don't mind," he said, flexing his hand impatiently. "And one of the branches."

"Oh!" Elizabeth turned away from him as fast as she could. She took an extra moment gathering up the items he needed, just long enough for her face to cool before turning back to him.

"Do you want these all the way across the doors?" He eyed the wide space over the doorframe.

"No. Perhaps just a couple in the middle. Since I have so few . . ." She hadn't meant it as a complaint, but he looked down and caught her eye.

"I said I'd cut you more today. I don't break my promises."

She couldn't look away from those eyes. He held her gaze, and she was caught, imprisoned in the intense blue that wouldn't let her go. "All right," she said because she couldn't think of what else to say.

He finally turned his attention back to the pine boughs, and Elizabeth caught hold of the doorframe as she fought to breathe again.

She was silent while he worked for a few minutes, until curiosity got the best of her. "I thought you said you might be leaving this morning?"

"I decided not to." He hammered a nail through the branch and into the wall, then looked to her for approval.

Elizabeth nodded, and he moved on to the next branch. The silence between them was bigger than this entire hotel. "Are you going to work for another ranch?" she finally asked.

The hammer slipped and Elizabeth winced as he caught his thumb. He mumbled something—likely something she was glad she didn't hear—and glared at his thumb.

"Are you all right?" she said after a moment.

"Yes. And no, I'm not working for another ranch. Not until spring." He spoke to the wall and not to her.

"Oh." Elizabeth ran her hands over her arms. Despite the fire nearby, she'd become chilled. She didn't dare ask him what work it was that awaited him in Cañon City, considering he didn't seem to want to discuss it. But she felt as if she needed to give him hope. After all, it might become something he liked, even if he didn't feel so optimistic about it right now. "I never expected to become a waitress. But I am now, and I'm learning to enjoy it."

Landon said nothing for a moment. He adjusted the pine bough he'd just hung, and then climbed down the ladder. "What do you think?" He gestured at his work.

Elizabeth lifted her eyes to take in his efforts. "I love it. Thank you. I'd like to add some bows, but I don't have those ready yet."

His jaw worked, and she feared she'd asked too much. "All right," he finally said.

"I can make them now," Elizabeth said, gathering up the velvet ribbon. "It won't take but a moment."

Landon sat in a nearby chair, and Elizabeth took that as his assent to wait while she fashioned the ribbon into bows. They were quiet as she worked. Then, out of nowhere, Landon spoke.

"This work I'm taking on is not something I'll ever learn to enjoy."

Elizabeth looked up at him. "How do you know? Have you done it before?"

"No," he said, a little forcefully as he sat up straighter. "And I'll be thankful to never do it again after this winter."

She blinked at him, trying to discern what sort of work he found so distasteful. It must be indoors. Colin despised indoor work after so many years on the ranch. Even mining felt too confining to him, and he'd grown sour and disagreeable the longer they'd stayed in California. "I know how much cowboys dislike working inside," she said.

He raised an eyebrow. "How would you know such a thing?"

"My husband. He worked on a ranch for several years." Elizabeth looked back at her ribbon. She disliked speaking of Colin. Although they'd had some pleasant moments together, most of her marriage had been a mixture of loneliness and fear. "You cowboys are all alike."

Mr. Cooper laughed, but it was short and lacked the mirth a laugh should have. "You—"

"This looks perfect!" Penny appeared between them, her hands clasped together in joy. "Elizabeth, you're a natural at decorating! You should have told me you were planning to start so early. Dora and I could have helped you. We might have even gotten some of the other girls to join in."

"I'm sorry, I got carried away. Do you really like it?" A warmth flooded Elizabeth's heart as Penny nodded.

"You know, you *must* hang mistletoe from the doorways. Can you imagine? Perhaps I should move our weddings inside. Then we could share a kiss under one of these doorways." Penny's face was alight as she gestured at the pine boughs over the dining-room doors.

"That's a wonderful idea," Elizabeth said. "I'm fashioning bows right now. Mr. Cooper is going to hang them for me."

"Isn't that kind of him?" Penny turned an eagle-eyed gaze onto Mr. Cooper, who stood and nodded to Penny. "I don't believe we've met." She glanced at Elizabeth, her eyes widening just slightly.

Elizabeth placed a hand over her mouth to keep from laughing. Penny reminded her of a girl she'd known in Denver, before her father had passed on—always the first to know the latest gossip and forever trying to match her friends to the eligible men in town.

She introduced Penny to Mr. Cooper, who offered a barely polite hello to Elizabeth's new friend. Elizabeth suspected his reaction had more to do with the obvious grin Penny flitted between Elizabeth and him than it did with his usual brooding manner.

"I must go . . . tend to the plants," Penny said. She gripped Elizabeth's hand and let go. "I'll find you later this morning."

Elizabeth watched her leave with a smile.

Mr. Cooper remained his silent, frowning self, but he shifted from foot to foot as if he wasn't certain what to do with himself. Elizabeth said nothing, but bit her lip to keep from grinning at his obvious discomfort. Instead, she fumbled with the bows and wished her heart would slow down. When she glanced up, Mr. Cooper was watching her with that intense gaze. She handed him the bows, and he turned to climb the ladder with them.

Elizabeth took a deep breath. Those eyes were trouble. *He* was trouble. But as much as she recognized that and knew she should stop him right now and find some other serviceable man to hang the bows, she didn't.

Instead, she prayed her brother would return soon, before she could get herself into another situation she'd wish she hadn't.

Chapter Eight

Landon dropped another armload of pine branches in front of the stone fireplace. That should do it. He'd cut an ungodly number of boughs, so many he didn't care to count. It had taken most of the afternoon, as he'd gone from tree to tree in order to make it less obvious that he'd taken so many. His arms ached, and his face was nearly frozen, but the look he knew he'd see on Mrs. Campbell's face kept him cutting and cutting.

It was a foolish thought, and he was well aware of it, and yet he hadn't bothered to stop thinking it.

She was most likely working right now, which left him with time. Time in which he should be resolving to leave for Cañon City. He'd already stayed longer than he'd intended.

Landon carried the saw down the hallway that passed the kitchen and led toward several other rooms whose purposes remained a mystery to him. At the end of the hall, a door led outside to a garden area that was empty and covered in snow this time of year. Landon crossed it and made his way to a shed that sat behind the hotel kitchen, which was where one of the bellboys had informed him the saw belonged.

He tugged on the door, but it wouldn't budge. Puzzled, he looked closer at the handle. It didn't appear to lock. He pulled again, and the door finally gave, flying open. He stepped inside, blinking in the dim light. The shed was larger than it had looked from outside. He strolled around the perimeter, searching for the right place. Just as he found it and had hung the saw from a little peg on the wall, the door shut and darkness enveloped the shed.

Landon spun around. From somewhere in the vicinity of the door, he could hear someone breathing. "Who's there?" he called into the dark.

"It's me, Elizabeth Campbell. I'm sorry. I didn't think anyone was in here."

Landon wasn't certain how it was possible, but he felt relieved and anxious at the same time. Of all the people who might wander into a shed filled with tools, Mrs. Campbell would have been the last person he expected. He could hear her tugging at the door.

"It won't open," she said.

"Here, let me get it. It sticks." He felt his way across the shed, brushing against her when he had apparently reached the door.

She stepped backward in a hurry. "I shouldn't have closed it. I didn't realize there were no windows."

Landon grunted his assent. All of his effort was going into pulling on the door handle, but the blasted thing wouldn't budge. He stopped for a moment, caught his breath, and tried again. Finally, after several minutes had passed, he turned and leaned against the door.

"Are we shut in here?" Elizabeth asked in a small voice.

He could just make out where she was standing, the faintest outlines of her darker shadow against that of the rest of the shed. "For now."

"We can't be. I'll be missed. And—and—it's freezing in here." She rubbed her hands up and down the sleeves that covered her arms.

"Why on earth would you come outside without a coat?" Although he'd seen her coat, and it wasn't even remotely warm enough for winter in this valley.

"I thought I'd only be out here for a few minutes. The spare cloak in the kitchen was gone, and I thought . . . I thought . . ." She trailed off, shivering.

Landon grumbled under his breath. He'd never heard anything so foolish in his life. But he shrugged out of his own coat and held it out to her. "Here."

She shook her head. "I couldn't possibly."

"Quit arguing and put it on."

"But you'll freeze without it." She dropped her gaze to the coat.

"I'll live. But you might not." It might have seen better days, but it was warm, which was the only thing that mattered in this weather.

She pushed her lips together and he half expected her to argue again. But she didn't. Instead, she took a couple of steps forward, and then turned around, pushing her arms into the sleeves.

"Thank you," she said as she turned around.

The sleeves dangled far past her hands, and the coat swallowed her whole. A rumpled angel. Landon couldn't help it—he laughed.

She smiled. "Do I look that ridiculous?"

"You look . . ." He didn't dare finish the sentence. Instead, he turned back to the door. Pulling on it was getting them nowhere. There had to be some other way.

"I didn't mean to come in here," Mrs. Campbell said. "The other girls sent me in search of spare silverware, and I looked in all the closets I found in the hotel, so I came out here and . . ."

"And you expected to find silverware in a shed?"

She pulled his coat tighter around herself. "I didn't. I just didn't know where else to look. I feel as if all I do is ask questions, so I thought that maybe, for once, I could do something without needing to run back and ask for more direction. And now look what I've done."

Landon felt the strangest desire to gather her into his arms and assure her it would all be fine. But instead he tugged uselessly on the door again. "We'll either figure a way out or someone will come looking for you."

"They can't." Her voice squeaked just a little.

"Why wouldn't they? You said yourself that you'll be missed."

"No, it's that I'll be in so much trouble if I'm found here."

He cocked his head, puzzled.

"With you," she added in a whisper.

"Ah." That made sense. Too much sense. "You couldn't possibly be found alone with someone like me. I understand."

"No, you don't—"

"I've heard enough. I'm good enough to do little chores for you, but too rough to spend time with." Fire pinched at his insides, dousing the hurt with anger that he'd kept bottled up for over a year. "I know how this works. I've done it before, believe it or not."

"What do you mean? I think you misunderstand—"

"I misunderstand nothing." He yanked harder at the handle, which began to splinter into his hand. He barely even felt it. All those feelings he'd pushed aside when Aimee turned down his proposal boiled up and over. "For someone without a penny to her name, you act awful high and mighty."

"How dare you!" Her words lashed out at him, so fast and ferocious that he took a step back from the door. "You don't know me. You don't know where I've come from or what I've lived through. And I did *not* mean anything so cruel when I said I couldn't be caught here with you. If you'd have let me speak, you'd know I must follow the rules of the hotel. And those rules include not spending time alone with a man. *Any* man. If we're found here, I could lose the position I don't even fully have yet. I need the wages I'm going to earn, since I am, as you so kindly pointed out, penniless."

She'd stepped closer and closer as she spoke until she was but a few inches from him. He had to look down to see her face. Even in the shadows, it was clear her angel face had gone red. She glared at him now, her hands on her hips and her breath coming fast.

Landon swallowed, all of his own anger vanished in the heat of hers. He didn't think she had such fury in her. "I misspoke."

"Hmmph," was the only sound she made in reply.

"I . . . apologize." The word scraped at his throat. He couldn't remember the last time he'd apologized to anyone.

She glared at him.

He threw his hands up in the air. "I don't know what else to say."

"How about you think before you assume the worst about someone in the future?" she said, her face still turned up and glaring at him. He wanted more than anything to run a finger down her cheek and watch her frown disappear.

Where had that thought come from? He took a step back from her before his mind left him completely. There was something she'd said, though, that bothered him. "What did you mean by 'what I've lived through'?"

She stood there a moment, and then her hands slowly drifted from her hips and her face took on a haunted look. "It's nothing."

And darned if that didn't make him even more curious. "You know why I'm here. Tell me, why are you? What made you come to a hotel in the middle of this valley, miles and miles from any real town?" He gestured around him, even though they couldn't see the valley inside this shed.

She wrapped her arms around herself and studied him a moment before speaking. "I came to find my brother. I had nowhere to go after I was widowed."

"And did you find him?"

She shook her head. "Not yet."

Silence settled between them. This wasn't the first time she'd mentioned being a widow, but the way she said it . . . it was as if it was an event that had happened to someone else. As if she held no emotion about it at all. He didn't know what to think of that.

"He's supposed to be on his way back here," she said. "I don't know if he'll be happy to see me."

Landon furrowed his brow. He couldn't imagine anyone being unhappy to see her. "I doubt that, Elizabeth."

Her eyes widened and the ghost of a smile crossed her lips, so quickly he thought he might have imagined it. "What did you call me?"

Too late, he'd realized his mistake. He should regret it. It was too familiar. It drew him that much closer to her. It would make it infinitely harder for him to make the decision he knew he needed to. He should apologize—again—and take it back.

But he didn't want to.

"Elizabeth suits you better than Mrs. Campbell," he said.

She ran her hands up and down her arms again, over his coat. Landon no longer felt the cold. Elizabeth lit up the entire room with warmth. Or perhaps he was delirious with fever. That certainly made more sense than anything else he'd done or thought or said today.

"We should try the door again," she said.

It was the last thing he wanted to do, but he obliged her and pulled on the handle again.

It opened immediately—to a person standing in the doorway.

Chapter Nine

Elizabeth gasped as Mr. Cooper stumbled backward. She blinked at the light from outside, but she could see well enough to recognize Genia. The relief that shot through her was so strong she thought she might crumple to the ground.

"Oh, thank goodness you're here," Genia said. "We couldn't imagine where you'd gotten off to. Why did you come to the—" She stopped speaking the second her eyes landed on Mr. Cooper. "Oh."

"This isn't . . . It isn't . . ." Elizabeth rushed out the door to Genia, her heart thumping in time to her pounding feet. "Please don't say anything to Mrs. Ruby. It was an accident. I didn't know Mr. Cooper was here, and I shut the door, and it refused to open again. I would never . . . Please don't say anything."

Genia's eyes were wide as she looked between Elizabeth and Mr. Cooper.

"She speaks the truth," he said, stepping out into the snow. "If you ladies will excuse me." And just like that, he was gone.

Elizabeth stared after him. What sort of man vanished like that, leaving a woman to defend herself alone?

"He's quite handsome. Hasn't he been eating at the counter?" Genia watched as Mr. Cooper disappeared into the hotel.

"Yes. And no. I mean, yes. He's utterly infuriating. And entirely without manners." Elizabeth crossed her arms.

Genia smiled. "And yet he gave you his coat. How unmannerly."

Elizabeth glanced down and groaned. She was still in the man's coat.

"Have no fear, your secret is safe with me." Genia pinched the fabric of the dirt-stained coat between her fingers. "However, you may want to take that off before we go back inside. Else Mrs. Ruby won't know what to think."

Elizabeth pulled Mr. Cooper's coat off. She immediately regretted it. Not only did the freezing air bite right through her dress, it felt as if he'd gone forever.

She held the coat out to Genia, who shook her head. "Oh, no. Returning that is all your responsibility. As much as I might like the excuse to talk to a cowboy like him, I don't think it's me he much cares to speak with."

Elizabeth sighed and held the coat to herself. Of course, now that Genia had mentioned it, she was looking forward to giving this coat back to him. And yet, she was still angry with him.

How was that possible?

They entered the hotel through the hallway door, which made it easy for Elizabeth to hide Mr. Cooper's coat in the laundry room before returning to the lunch counter. Genia agreed to tell Mrs. Ruby that Elizabeth had been found.

Settling herself behind the lunch counter, which was beginning to fill with men who wanted dinner, Elizabeth tried to rein in her thoughts. If Mr. Cooper—Landon, she supposed she should call him, although that would be admitting she desired to get to know him better—came in here for his own meal while she was working, she might burst from the confusion that clouded her mind.

She managed to greet customers and take their orders. She even laughed and talked with the ones she was learning preferred conversation. It took her mind off Landon—who never came in to eat. By the end of the dinner shift, her feet hurt, her back ached, and she was smiling as she'd never smiled before.

As she wiped down the lunch counter, she realized it was because she enjoyed this work. It was hard, but she fit in here. She was more at ease in this hotel than she'd ever been in the mining camp. She was making friends.

She wanted to stay. That meant no more putting this job at risk for a cowboy who expected the worst of her, no matter how many pine boughs he hung for her or coats he lent her.

LATER THAT NIGHT, ELIZABETH slipped quietly into the room she shared with Sarah, Landon's coat balled up in her arms.

"Elizabeth?"

Elizabeth leaned her head against the door. She'd hoped Sarah would be asleep, as she had been by this time each night since Elizabeth had arrived. Sarah ignited the lamp, and as it flickered to life, Elizabeth turned to find her roommate sitting up in bed.

"Why are you coming in so late?" Sarah asked as she squinted at Elizabeth. "And what do you have in your hands? Are those dirty linens?"

"I . . . no." Elizabeth forced her feet to move toward the small wardrobe in the closet. "It's a coat. I found it. Downstairs."

"Who does it belong to?"

"I'm not certain." Elizabeth's face flamed as she spoke the lie. It was for her own good, she reminded herself as she pushed Landon's coat in the corner of the wardrobe. She'd done nothing wrong by going to the shed, but Sarah, as head waitress, might feel compelled to inform Mrs. Ruby. She'd return the coat to Landon tomorrow, and no one aside from Genia would be any the wiser.

"Why did you bring it up here? You could've left it at the front desk for its owner to claim it."

Elizabeth took a deep breath and turned to face Sarah, who had unbraided her hair only to replait it. "You're right. I didn't know what to do with it, but I'll bring it down in the morning."

"How are you finding the lunch counter?" Sarah smiled at Elizabeth as she tied the ends of her hair again.

Thankful for the change in subject, Elizabeth forced herself to breathe and moved to untie her apron. "It's busy, but I enjoy it. I never realized how much I like being occupied."

Sarah leaned forward eagerly. "May I share a secret with you?"

Elizabeth paused, wondering what sort of secret Sarah might have. She hung her apron as she considered it. "Certainly," she finally said.

"Mrs. Ruby told me she has high hopes for you. Apparently your work at the lunch counter has impressed her. You might find yourself moving to the dining room come January." Sarah wrapped her arms around her knees and grinned at Elizabeth.

"She said that?" The news was startling enough to remove Landon from Elizabeth's thoughts for the first time since she'd finished the dinner service.

"She did."

Elizabeth shook her head. "I can hardly believe it. I never thought I'd be working here, much less doing so successfully." She sat at the dressing table to take down her hair.

"Don't let on that I told you, though," Sarah said, inching back down under the bedcovers.

"I won't say a word." Elizabeth glanced at her roommate, wondering at how lucky she was to not only have found work here that she enjoyed, but friends too. She hadn't had a real friend in years, not since Colette at the ranch. "Thank you."

"I'll leave the lamp on," Sarah said in a drowsy voice.

Elizabeth turned back to the small mirror that sat on the vanity and unpinned the small gray hat that sat at the crown of her head. As she pulled it away, she studied her face and wondered how Landon saw her. He was awfully quick to assume she thought so little of him. What had he said? He'd "done this before," whatever that meant. Her only guess was that a woman had spurned him in the past. It had touched a nerve. The heat of his anger could have seared her in the cold air of the shed. He'd apologized, for which she was grateful, but it was hard to shake such a reaction. She'd spent too many years dodging that exact sort of rage from Colin.

Colin had never apologized.

Elizabeth paused in the middle of removing a pin from her hair. Landon had done the one thing Colin never had. Did that make it any different? People got angry from time to time, the sensible part of herself thought. It was how they handled that anger that mattered. Colin had thrown things and said terrible words to her before storming out into the night. Landon had done nothing like that.

Still, it made her nervous. It *all* made her uneasy, everything from the way he looked at her to how much she looked forward to returning his coat. She could make all the resolutions she wanted here in her room, alone but for Sarah.

But somehow, she doubted she'd remain true to them tomorrow.

Chapter Ten

L andon stood in the hotel lobby, choking on how much Christmas was all around him. Elizabeth had been busy since he'd last seen her yesterday afternoon. He'd made himself scarce, forgoing meals and eating the usual foods he'd brought for his ride to Cañon City. He was supposed to be there in two days, and yet here he was, still at this hotel.

And now he was surrounded by an entire forest of pine, more red velvet than he'd ever seen in his life, festive berries, gold doodads that hung from every bough, and even a few ribbons that dangled from the front desk. All that was missing was a tree.

He expected it all to press in on him, making it hard to breathe, but it didn't. Instead, he found himself smiling like a man who'd gone daft in the head, as memories of his mother and the ranch where he'd grown up flooded his mind. He could see it like it was yesterday. The way the family they'd worked for invited all the servants and ranch hands into the house for Christmas dinner, how they'd taken special care to ensure that he was included with their own children on Christmas morning, how his mother had enjoyed watching him open gifts.

A strange sort of *missing* enveloped him from head to toe. He hadn't had family since he was sixteen, when his mother died and he went off to work on another ranch. Since then, there had been no Christmas dinners, no gifts, and certainly no trees. But it wasn't the lack of those things that caused this feeling—it was the spirit of it all. The joy and laughter, the warmth and the love of family. The pang of it wrenched his heart open, and he had to look away from the decorations.

What he wouldn't give to feel that way again. To have his own home lit up with joy and love, and yes, even a bunch of silly pine boughs that really belonged outside.

And maybe it could happen. One day. But first, he had to get to Cañon City. He rubbed his face, trying to iron out his thoughts. It was clear that if he chose not to take this step, he'd never have enough to start up his own ranch. And he didn't know if he could go on, year in and year out, working for other people and knowing his own dreams were so far out of reach.

It was one winter. That was all. One winter of rustling enough cattle to sell to men greedy enough not to ask any questions. If only he could set aside the rock that seemed to form in his stomach every time he thought of it. It was easy money. Redmond and the others were counting on him . . . but they didn't need him to proceed. In fact, they'd each make more without him, even if it meant they'd have to work a little harder.

They wouldn't go out until January. He still had some time, but he'd need to let them know. If he didn't show his face in Cañon City in two days, Redmond would assume he was out. He needed to buy more time.

He'd wire Redmond. That was the perfect solution.

Mind made up, Landon peered into the room that housed the lunch counter. He couldn't take another night of salt pork, but he also couldn't face Elizabeth. She'd returned his coat through the desk clerk that morning. He wanted to thank her, but he didn't dare.

There she was, laughing as she spoke with one of her customers. Landon's hand curled around the doorframe. He wanted to be the one in that seat, making her laugh.

But he couldn't. Not with what he had planned. If he let this take its natural course, he'd find himself leaving her behind very soon. Or he wouldn't go at all. He wasn't sure which one was worse. If only he had that land now. If he had a house, and a way to provide for someone like Elizabeth.

But he didn't, and she deserved better than a man like him. One whose only serious relationship had ended in a woman spurning him and reminding him exactly who he was. One who planned to spend the rest of the winter stealing from the very people who'd given him work over the years.

It was best he left her alone. She was likely still mad at him anyway, after the way he'd spoken to her in the shed.

He turned and went upstairs to a dinner of salt pork. After that, he'd walk down to the depot to send a telegram to Redmond. And in a day or two, he'd leave.

Alone.

Chapter Eleven

Elizabeth held the tiny china dog in her hands. Her mother had collected little keepsakes like this. For the first time, she wondered what had happened to them. She hadn't thought of them in years. She wanted so badly to buy it, but she only had a small amount of money. And even that wasn't really hers. Mrs. McFarland had caught her this morning and given her a few dollars. "An advance on your wages. For trinkets you might wish to buy for Christmas gifts." She'd smiled at Elizabeth in a motherly fashion, and Elizabeth could have cried right then and there.

Instead, she'd come to the general store and mercantile across the railroad tracks. It was the only shop in Crest Stone, which one couldn't really call a town. At least not yet, but if Penny and Dora were correct, it would be a town by this time next year. And that was why her brother was coming back, she'd learned. To help build the town. He hadn't arrived yet, and Penny was getting antsy. Christmas—and her wedding—was in less than five days, and if Monroe's wife, Emma Hartley, wasn't there to celebrate it, Penny wasn't sure what she would do.

Elizabeth sighed and placed the little dog back on the shelf, thinking about how much she had missed.

"He's adorable, don't you think?" a woman said from behind her.

"My mother collected these," Elizabeth said. She turned to find the proprietress of the store standing behind her, radiant blonde hair pulled up into a neat chignon and a warm smile on her face.

"She had good taste, then," the woman said. "I'm Caroline Drexel. You must be a new employee of the hotel."

"Elizabeth Campbell. And you're right, except I'm not fully employed yet, Mrs. Drexel."

"Please call me Caroline. I used to be a Gilbert Girl. Until I met my husband, that is." As the woman spoke, Elizabeth remembered Penny and Dora mentioning her as a friend, the one who had married her husband while he was jailed.

"I hope to be," Elizabeth said, unable to keep the enthusiasm from her voice. "If I pass Mrs. Ruby's muster."

Caroline smiled again. "She's tough, but very fair. And quite kind, once you get to know her."

"Ah." Elizabeth wasn't certain what else to say. To be honest, Mrs. Ruby intimidated her. "I'm searching for Christmas gifts. For my new friends. And my brother."

"I know most everyone at the hotel. You must tell me who you're looking for, and I'll help you."

Elizabeth rattled off the names of the girls who had been especially friendly toward her. Caroline led her around the store, pointing out various items until Elizabeth had her hands full.

"And now for your brother. Does he work at the hotel?"

"No. He did, but . . . not now." Elizabeth fumbled her words.

"Does he live on a ranch nearby?" Caroline asked.

"No . . ." Elizabeth chewed on her lip. She hadn't told Penny or Dora who her brother was. Adelaide knew, but she was the only one. Maybe being at the hotel made it feel too close, like the disappointment she feared from him would somehow filter through to them. But Caroline was here, at the general store, and not at the hotel. And it would be nice to tell someone. "He built the hotel."

If Caroline was surprised, she was too polite to show it. "Mr. Hartley is your brother?"

Elizabeth nodded. "I haven't seen him in years."

"Then you must choose something extra special."

The door to the store opened, and wind blew in, whipping Elizabeth's skirts around her legs.

"Pardon me. I'll attend to this customer and return as soon as I can." Caroline bustled away.

Elizabeth smoothed down her skirt with one hand while clutching her gifts with the other—until a man's voice made her stop still.

"I'm looking for more of those little gold baubles. For the hotel."

Had he seen her? She was half-hidden behind some shelving. She peered out—and he immediately spotted her. A moment passed, and finally he nodded at her.

Elizabeth gave him a quick smile. She wasn't sure how to act. She was happy to see him, although she knew she shouldn't be. She busied herself with placing her purchases on the counter. Which turned out to be the wrong decision.

"Mrs. Campbell." He was beside her. Her formal name felt awkward to hear in his voice now. The wild part of her wished he'd call her Elizabeth again.

"Mr. Cooper." She didn't dare look up at him. If she did, she feared she wouldn't be able to look away. And she certainly didn't dare call him Landon, not when he'd reverted to addressing her as Mrs. Campbell. And especially not when she needed desperately to keep distance between them.

But he said nothing else, and she felt compelled to end the silence. "You haven't left yet."

"I haven't."

She moved a few items across the counter.

"Are you still angry with me?" he asked.

Elizabeth swallowed. Was that what he thought? "I should be, with the way you disappeared." She glanced up at him out of the corner of her eye. "But no, I'm not angry."

He said nothing, but his eyes remained on her.

Her heart pounded so hard she could feel it in her throat. "Won't your new job miss you?"

"I've sent a telegram."

She wanted so badly to ask him why he remained here in Crest Stone, but wasn't certain which answer she wanted to hear. "I'm purchasing Christmas gifts," she said for lack of any other thing to say.

He was silent. Elizabeth wished he would say something. Anything. If he didn't, she'd be forced to look up at him to discern his reaction. She rearranged her items on the polished wooden counter to busy her hands.

"We have a few more, but this is all." Caroline bustled out from the door that must have led to a room they used for storage. She set five gold Christmas ornaments on the counter in front of Landon. "Did you wish to purchase all of them?"

Elizabeth stared at the ornaments. "Why are you buying those?" He was the last person she'd suspect of being awash in the spirit of Christmas.

He cleared his throat and her eyes drifted up to him of their own accord.

"I presumed you needed a few more to place on a tree." He looked everywhere but at her.

Elizabeth placed a hand against her heart, which felt ready to burst from her body. He was purchasing them for her. For a tree she hadn't yet asked if anyone at the hotel might cut for her. "I don't know what to say. You don't have to buy them."

"I want to," he said, a bit gruffly.

His irritation brought a smile to her face. And then she knew. He might have the manner and the rough exterior of a cowboy, but inside, he was as soft as the snow that lay on the ground. "Then by all means, I wouldn't presume to stop you."

He looked down then, rubbing a hand through his hair. "In that case, I'll take them all," he said to Caroline.

"Thank you," Elizabeth said. "They'll look lovely on the tree."

Landon drummed his fingers on the counter, not looking at her.

"You don't accept gratitude easily, do you?" Elizabeth said.

"I haven't had much opportunity," he replied, finally meeting her eyes again. He held her there for a few seconds before looking down to remove money from his pocket.

Caroline wrapped the ornaments and placed each one in a box before taking Landon's money and wishing him a good day.

"I'll carry these back," he said before replacing his hat and nodding at each of them. And then he was gone.

Elizabeth was left with the strangest tangle of feelings. "I cannot believe he did that."

"That man is in love with you," Caroline said as she began wrapping Elizabeth's purchases.

Elizabeth's hand dropped to her stomach. *Love.* She thought she might be sick. Caroline barely knew either of them. Surely she was reading Landon wrong.

"He's the most uncouth, sullen man I've ever met," she finally said. "He comes all the way over here to buy those ornaments, and yet he lacks the most basic sort of manners at times." *And he's a cowboy*, she wanted to add, but she knew that would only make sense to herself.

A smile twitched Caroline's lips as she tied a string around the small bottle of perfume Elizabeth had chosen for Penny. "Men are strange creatures." She reached for another sheet of brown paper and looked up at Elizabeth. "Just be careful if you choose to allow him to continue in this manner. Both your brother and my friend Emma paid for their relationship with their jobs. As did I and my husband. Mr. McFarland might be soft when it comes to love, but even he must follow the rules of the Gilbert Company. And the company doesn't stand for any sort of scandal."

Elizabeth dug her fingers into her coat. Scandal was the last thing she wanted. She'd had enough of the ups and downs of love to last her the rest of her life. All she craved now was stability. Dull, sensible stability.

"He isn't courting me," she said.

"That's what you might think," Caroline replied, handing her the box in which she'd placed Elizabeth's gifts. "Now, did you find anything for your brother?"

Elizabeth shook her head and allowed Caroline to show her multiple items. But her mind couldn't stay put on her brother and a gift for him, not when it kept wandering back to Landon. He was a conundrum, that was the only thing about which she was certain. Handsome, yet rough around the edges. Kind, yet gruff. Thoughtful, yet lacking in manners. He was night and day from Colin. Even the way in which he angered was different.

It was enough to make her think that maybe not all cowboys were the same.

Chapter Twelve

The telegram was short and to the point.

Be here by Christmas Eve. R.

Landon had folded it up and placed it in his pocket. It would do him good to remember what awaited him in Cañon City. He stood to make a considerable amount of money, and that's what he needed to keep in mind. Money that would set him up for a future in which he was his own boss. In which he had his own spread. And in which he could live comfortably for the rest of his life.

Alone.

He tapped his fingers on the lunch counter. Not necessarily alone. Once he had his affairs in order, he'd be in a position to take a wife and start a family. Of course, in every vision he'd had of that future lately, the wife always looked the same—hair the color of the great sand dunes that rose on the other side of these mountains, eyes nearly as dark as night, and a face with the perpetual glow that befitted an angel.

No woman wants to marry an outlaw.

Landon ground his teeth together. He wouldn't be an outlaw forever. Only briefly. It was a means to an end, and that was all. She wouldn't even need to know about it. Not if he was careful.

He was getting ahead of himself. Elizabeth had barely spoken to him save for those few minutes in the general store yesterday. He wondered if she had avoided him as much as he'd avoided her. But for all of that effort, it was as if they hadn't spent a moment apart when he saw her yesterday.

Now he found himself at the lunch counter, knowing full well she might be here.

He glanced down the length of the counter, looking past two of the other waitresses who often worked there. Just as he was about to give up hope, Eliz-

abeth rushed in, tying her apron the same way she had the first time he'd met
her.

Sense smacked him upside the head. What was he doing here? He should
go. Nothing good could come of this. And yet he remained fixed in his seat,
wondering when she might see him.

She finally glanced up, her eyes immediately landing on him. In less than
a couple of seconds, she was in front of him, smiling as always. No one but an
angel could possibly smile this much. It wasn't natural.

"Good afternoon, Landon," she said.

If he thought her voice was musical before, hearing her say his Christian
name was like the heavens had opened up to a chorus of angels just like Elizabeth. He should reply, say "Good afternoon" or something similar to her, but
he was struck dumb.

"The chef has chicken soup today. Could I get you a bowl?" she asked.

He nodded, not trusting his voice to actually speak. She left to put in his order, and he relaxed a little. Until she returned, that is, with a bowl in one hand
and a plate in the other. She set both dishes in front of him.

"I brought you a slice of spice cake too. I hope you like it."

"Thank you," he finally choked out, and then immediately brought a spoon-
ful of soup to his mouth so he wouldn't be required to say anything else.

Her smile widened, as if his thanks was everything she needed. The soup
scorched his tongue, but he swallowed it anyway and pressed his napkin to his
mouth.

"I'm sorry. It's from right off the stove. Here, let me get you some water."
Elizabeth poured him a glass that he downed in one quick swallow. She immediately poured him another. "When it cools, you'll have to tell me how you like
it. We're considering asking the chef to make it for the Christmas wedding luncheon."

Landon nodded. "Yes," was all he said.

"Good." Elizabeth set her water pitcher down and reached for a towel to
wipe off the counter. "The chef balked at how many pies Penny wished to have.
I volunteered to bake them myself, as did Mrs. McFarland, and that seemed to
appease him some."

Landon stared at her as she cleaned off the counter. She certainly wasn't being paid to cook or bake, and yet here she was, willing to spend her free time

baking for another girl's wedding. "Do you . . . do you bake much?" He winced inwardly at the awkwardness of his question. Conversation had never come naturally to him, particularly when he hoped to give his best impression.

His best impression. He didn't dare think any further on *that*.

"I used to," she said wistfully. "Sometimes for the few other women in camp when they were recovering from childbirth. But mostly for myself."

Landon stirred his spoon around in his soup. What sort of man wouldn't appreciate a pie or some fresh bread? He watched Elizabeth from the corner of his eye. This wasn't the first time she'd mentioned something strange about her deceased husband. He felt there was more to the story, but couldn't figure out the right way to ask.

Elizabeth finished her cleaning and slid the towel through a drawer handle behind the counter. "I wish to thank you again for purchasing those ornaments. That was very thoughtful."

He nodded as he lifted his eyes to her. She stood there, looking impossibly demure and perfect in that waitress's uniform, with a smile that was only for him. It made him want to beg that shopkeeper woman for more Christmas baubles just so he could have her look at him that way again and again. "You're welcome." The words stumbled from his mouth, but they made her smile even broader.

"I'll take that bowl for you." She slid a hand around the edge of his empty soup bowl. "What do you think? Is it worthy of a wedding lunch on Christmas Day?"

Landon nodded again, and that seemed to make her happy.

"Oh, good. I'll be sure to tell Penny and Dora what you thought." She turned and made her way toward a small tub of dirty dishes that sat on the floor at the other end of the counter. She paused for a moment to talk to another customer, and her face crinkled into a laugh.

He didn't deserve someone as good as Elizabeth. Aimee had certainly reminded him of that. He was nothing but a ranch hand, spending days outside in the sun chasing down other men's cattle. And come January, he'd be something even lower—a rustler of those same animals. Maybe one day, he'd at least *appear* deserving of a kind, gentle woman like Elizabeth, even if he wasn't.

So why couldn't he simply let her go? Why did he do fool-headed things like buying her Christmas ornaments? Or letting her scare up cake for him? He couldn't stay away, even though he knew it would only lead to trouble and a broken heart.

But did it have to?

He'd have money soon. He'd at least carry the appearance of a man who deserved the world, even if he was still the same man at heart. Landon drew his hands across his face, trying to make his thoughts line up in some way that made sense. What if he asked her to wait? Would she? Could he live with himself if he did?

She glanced over her shoulder at him, and her smile grew more brilliant than any of the gold Christmas decorations that surrounded them.

As wrong as it was, he couldn't let her go.

Chapter Thirteen

Elizabeth shivered against the wind that bit at her face. It had grown more fierce as of late, coming down from the mountains that towered over the hotel as if it were on a mission to race across the valley as quickly as possible. Her father would have said that such a wind bode ill weather to come.

But the sun shone, as weak as it was, and it wasn't snowing even a bit at the moment. She'd come outside for some fresh air and a little exercise. One could only stay cooped up inside for so long without needing to see the sun.

And so she wrapped her coat more tightly around herself and thanked God for her hood and a good pair of wool gloves. Maybe if she continued working at the hotel, she could save some money for a nicer coat, one that would not only keep her warmer but would also look as if it belonged to a woman of a decent station, and not one who'd lived such a miserable life in a mining camp that she'd actually felt a tiny spark of relief when her husband had died.

She made her way through the ankle-deep snow, her face turned up to the sun each time the wind gave her a moment. It was silent outside the hotel, the sort of silence that only comes with a fresh blanket of snowfall. It was as if the usual sounds of the world had been muffled, and the only one allowed was the wind cutting through the branches. And a *thwack-thwack-thwack* from somewhere closer to the creek.

Elizabeth stilled. It sounded as if something was hitting a tree. She moved carefully through the snow to what Genia had told her was an old wagon trail that cut through the tree line to the creek. The creek itself was entirely frozen, but that sound continued somewhere off to Elizabeth's right.

She followed the creek for a short ways until a figure came into view behind a stand of aspen. It was a man, swinging an axe at a pine tree, over and over. Elizabeth squinted through the sunlight. She recognized that coat, smudged with dirt and grass and smelling of campfire smoke.

It was Landon.

She hurried toward him as he swung the final stroke that felled the tree. It came down, crashing through its neighbors and sending snow blowing through the wind. Elizabeth held an arm up in front of her face to keep the icy flakes from hitting her skin. When she looked again, Landon had dropped the axe to the ground and was pulling the tree by its trunk across the snow. He stopped when he saw her.

"Is that . . .? Are you . . .?" She couldn't seem to form a sentence.

"For Christmas," he said abruptly. "For the hotel."

For me, she thought, and she suddenly felt too warm in her old, threadbare coat. "Thank you. Do you need assistance? I could fetch one of the kitchen boys to help you haul this back up to the hotel."

"No need." He adjusted his grip on the tree and picked up the axe with his free hand.

"Well, I could at least carry that for you." She took the few steps that stood between them and pulled the axe from his hand. It was heavier than she'd thought it would be, but she smiled at him and gripped the thing with both hands.

"I thought this was a fair size for the lobby." He nodded at the tree. "Large, but not too much so."

Elizabeth inspected the pine. "It's perfect. It'll look lovely in that space near the front windows." She shifted the axe to one hand to run the other over the tree's needles. "No one's cut a tree for me before. And I've always wanted one."

When she glanced up, Landon was watching her, curiosity etched across his face.

She sighed. As much as she didn't wish to speak of Colin, she'd brought this explanation upon herself by mentioning it. "My husband didn't much care for Christmas. He thought it a waste of time and effort to cut down a tree." She figured it would be better to keep the diatribe that usually accompanied such a request to herself. No one had ever made her feel so insignificant as her own husband had.

"It isn't a waste of time if it makes you happy," Landon said, irritation slicing through his voice. "Your former husband sounds like a man who didn't much care for anyone's happiness but his own." He paused, and added, "I overstepped."

Elizabeth didn't know what to say to that—any of it. He was right about Colin. He was right about overstepping. And she wasn't at all sure how she felt about any of it, especially the noticeable lack of an apology. Somehow she doubted Landon ever gave an apology for anything he wasn't truly sorry for. So she swallowed and took the axe into both hands again before saying, "Shall we bring this tree up to the hotel?"

He nodded and began to haul the tree down the creek toward the wagon path. Elizabeth trailed behind him, trying to discern what all of this meant. The man was awfully forthright—when he actually spoke, that was. She had so many questions for him, if she could get him to answer in more than just a couple of words. Who was this woman who'd hurt him so badly before? Why was he still here when a job awaited him in Cañon City? What *was* this job? And what of his family? She knew none of the answers, although if she were to be honest with herself, she knew exactly why he was still here.

But the thought frightened her as much as it sent joy spreading from her fingertips to her toes. Even though he had already proven how different he was from Colin, how could she know for certain that he wouldn't change later? Colin had been nothing but gentle and loving with her until they were married and moved to California. Then he'd turned into a man who was angry at the world. And that anger drove him to drink and gamble every cent they had, made him hurl insults at her so frequently she strove to avoid him, and ultimately found him dead in a mining accident he'd caused.

How could she ever trust another cowboy again, when she'd experienced what she had?

But how could she deny the feelings that were growing inside her each time Landon so much as glanced at her? Perhaps if she got to know him better, it would make everything more clear. If she could ask him the questions that pinched at her mind, then maybe she'd know for certain.

Chapter Fourteen

It was late by the time the tree had dried enough to be set up in the lobby. Landon lost count of how many times the needles had pricked his fingers and how often the sap had dripped down the backs of his hands, but it was done. He stepped back and admired his work. To be honest, he was more interested in how Elizabeth would react when she saw it tomorrow. He didn't want to miss that, and if he hoped to be awake early enough to see it, he needed to find his way to bed soon.

Only a couple of other guests remained in the lobby at this time of the evening. Landon crossed to the stairs and made his way up to the second floor. The area that overlooked the lobby was empty save for one woman, standing on a ladder.

Elizabeth.

Landon's heart almost stopped when that ladder teetered just slightly to the left. But Elizabeth righted it and went right back to hanging something green over the doorway to one of the rooms. Why in the name of all that was good was she doing this herself? She'd had the sense to ask him to hang those pine boughs downstairs, but now she climbed a ladder on her own? He strode toward her, impatient to get her off that ladder before she fell and hurt herself.

He was just a couple of steps away when the ladder tilted again. But this time, it kept going sideways, down toward the floor—and Elizabeth with it. She gave a startled cry, and that jolted Landon into action. He covered those last couple of steps as if they were but a tiny hop, just in time to catch her as she went down. With one arm wrapped under her waist and the other behind her knees, he held tight to her as she grabbed his neck.

The fear melted from her eyes as she looked up at him. It lasted but a second, but it felt like an eternity. She was safe because of him. And if he could make it that way forever, he would.

"Landon," she whispered.

He realized he was still holding on to her as if she were falling, and he quickly set her down on her feet. She stumbled a little, and he caught her arm. "Are you all right?"

"I think so." She pressed her free hand to her heart. "How did you get here just in time?"

"I don't know," he said as he took in the flush on her face and the delicate fingers pressed to her apron. "I suppose I knew angels can't really fly."

She tilted her head. "What do you mean?"

Warmth flooded his face. What a ridiculous thing to say. "Nothing. What were you doing up there?"

"Hanging mistletoe. It's not actual mistletoe, but it is a sprig of greenery with red berries. I found some growing along the creek." She glanced down at his hand that still clutched her arm.

He should let her go. It was late, and while most of the hotel had gone to bed, it was entirely possible that someone could walk by them. But instead of dropping her arm entirely, he found his fingers moving down her arm to her hand. It was small and soft in his, which was calloused from years of work outside.

She drew in a sharp breath, but she didn't move away from him. And so he let his hand remain curled around hers.

"I should apologize for what I said to you the other day," she said, her eyes on their hands. "In the shed, when I said you were the same as any man who worked on a ranch."

He raised his eyebrows but said nothing.

"My husband was a ranch hand, and he was . . . not particularly kind. And so I've always had it in my head that his behavior came from those years he spent in the company of other men, driving cattle and the like. But I fear I was wrong. I owe you an apology."

Her words cut into him, somewhere deep inside, a place where he hid his worst faults and fears, where he'd tucked away the cruel words Aimee had said to him. If this beautiful woman with the tender heart believed he was more than a poor cowboy, then perhaps he was. He gripped her hand tighter, and she looked up at him, her eyes wide with trust.

And yet, he was planning to keep the truth from her.

"You don't owe me anything," he said.

She raised her other hand and touched his cheek, a slight graze of the fingertips that sent his head spinning. "What is it that makes you so disbelieving of any kind words spoken to you?" she asked.

Landon couldn't piece together two words with her hand on his face. He gripped her other wrist gently, and she stopped. "Perhaps because they aren't true."

"But they are," she insisted. "You have a kind heart, even if you believe you don't. Even if someone else told you otherwise."

Would a man with a kind heart be planning to make money stealing other men's cattle? "You don't know everything about me," he said.

"Then tell me."

Her face was so close to his. Just a few inches. He could see her eyes tracing his face, feel the pulse in her wrist, see her breath quickening as he searched her face . . . for what? For proof she was speaking lies? Or for permission to close that distance between them and finally press his lips against hers?

"Tell me," she said again.

He wasn't good at words, and so he said nothing. Instead he moved closer to her, inch by inch until she closed her eyes. He could kiss her right now, and he wanted to, badly.

You aren't good enough. The thought curled through his mind, reaching through him until he stopped. Up close, she was even more beautiful, and if he kissed her, it could not only ruin her, but turn him into the worst sort of man—one who stole a heart under a pretense.

With every part of him feeling as if it were weighed down with lead, he let her go and stepped away.

Elizabeth's eyes fluttered open. She reached for the wall and gripped the doorframe. "You didn't tell me."

Landon was still attempting to discern the meaning behind her words when a voice sounded from behind him.

"Oh, my. Elizabeth, are you all right?" A round woman—a Mrs. Ruby, he believed—came bustling past him toward Elizabeth and the downed ladder.

Elizabeth stirred, taking her eyes from him to the woman, and she instantly stood straighter. "I'm not hurt. I was attempting to hang some berries over the parlor door, and the ladder slid out from underneath me."

Mrs. Ruby took her arm and held it out as if she were inspecting her charge. Then she glanced back to Landon.

"Mr. Cooper was passing by and was kind enough to help me up," Elizabeth said, her cheeks coloring.

Mrs. Ruby narrowed her eyes at Landon. He tried his best to look as if he hadn't just been contemplating kissing Elizabeth. It must have worked, because the woman said nothing. Instead she returned to fussing over her employee.

"It's past time for you to be in your room," she said.

"Oh! I must've lost track of the hour. I'm so sorry." Elizabeth's voice held an edge of desperation.

Landon wanted to step in for her. To tell Mrs. Ruby that Elizabeth had done nothing wrong. And he wanted to ensure Elizabeth he'd hang those troublesome berries for her tomorrow, but the words stopped up in his throat. Instead, he nodded at both women—neither of whom appeared to see him—and inched away until he was around the corner and headed down the south wing toward his room.

He fumbled with the key in his door. Elizabeth had his mind all addled. She kept asking him to confide in her. What if he did? What if he told her everything, from his dreams of owning his own ranch to the methods he was being forced to take if he wanted to do so? She'd be appalled, that much was for sure.

But maybe she'd understand, even if she didn't approve. Or perhaps she wouldn't, and he'd lose her forever.

He sighed as the door swung open. If he told her, there would be no taking it back. And if he didn't, could he live with the knowledge that he hadn't been entirely truthful with her?

Landon didn't know the answer. All he knew was that he wished he'd kissed her anyway.

Chapter Fifteen

Elizabeth hardly slept. After waking up for about the tenth time, she finally rose and left so she wouldn't awaken Sarah. Uncertain as to the actual time, she had the feeling it was very early morning. She made her way downstairs, hopeful she could find something to occupy her time before the breakfast shift she was scheduled to serve.

The lobby was empty. Even the desk clerk had disappeared off to somewhere. But something was different...

Elizabeth paused, and then gasped. The tree Landon had cut down yesterday stood tall and proud in the usual empty space between the hotel doors and the gathering of chairs around the fireplace nearest the dining room. Its lofty branches reached out, and it filled the room with such a lovely scent. She almost felt like crying, she was so happy to see it. Even without decoration, it made the room so much warmer and more homelike. Her heart ached as memories of childhood Christmases with both her parents and Monroe flitted through her mind. There weren't many—not so many she could remember well, at least—but each one was precious to her.

She clasped her hands together in front of her, already dreaming of how she'd decorate the tree. Perhaps the other girls would help her. Maybe Landon would look on, that sullen look finally erased for good as the Christmas spirit took over.

Landon.

She shivered when she thought of him and how close they were last night. How very, very close she had come to letting him kiss her. And she wouldn't have stopped him, either, even though he never explained himself. It was almost embarrassing to remember how wanton she'd acted, now, in the quiet of early morning. But she knew, deep down in her heart, that if she had it to do over again, she wouldn't change a thing.

But what would she do if he never opened up to her?

Elizabeth sighed and left the beautiful tree she knew he'd put up for her. How could a man be so thoughtful and so closed off at the same time? And he'd disappeared yet again without so much as a word to either herself or Mrs. Ruby. She hurried back to the lunch counter and took inventory of all the items she knew they'd need for a successful breakfast service. Someone must've stocked the counter last night, as everything was in place.

At a loss for what else to do, Elizabeth wandered into the kitchen. A few of the kitchen boys were up and beginning breakfast preparations, but nothing was ready for the hotel staff to eat yet. She took the spare cloak from the peg near the door and stepped outside.

The wind whipped her hair from the loose chignon she'd pulled it into. She pulled the hat from her head before it loosened from its pins and flew off into the trees. It was small enough she could put it into one of the pockets that had been sewn into the cloak. Perhaps there was something to what her father had always said about the wind coming down from the mountains.

Elizabeth blinked into the flurries that stung her face. Tucking her chin to her chest, she walked along the rear of the hotel and through the snow that now came up mid-calf.

"I fear there's a storm coming," a voice said from somewhere in front of her.

Elizabeth looked up. She had made it to the garden—such as it was in this weather. Penny stood there, her curls dancing around the edge of her hood and her face pink with cold.

"That's what my father would have said." Elizabeth shivered and tucked her hands deeper into the pockets of the cloak. She'd thought coming out here might clear her head, but instead, she felt as if she were fighting to even breathe.

"I couldn't sleep. I'm worried." Penny's face looked pinched as snow landed on her eyelashes. She blinked it away. "Ben is due in today. What if the routes are canceled because of the snow?"

Elizabeth chewed on her lower lip. It was certainly a possibility, especially if the weather didn't improve. And Christmas was only three days away. "Monroe hasn't arrived yet, either."

Penny nodded and then raised her eyebrows. "Monroe?"

"My brother," Elizabeth said after taking a deep breath.

"Monroe Hartley is your brother? Emma's husband?" Penny tugged her own coat closer to her as she spoke.

Elizabeth nodded.

"Oh, for the love of Christmas, Elizabeth! Why didn't you say that before? Here we've been speaking of him as if you'd never met him." If Penny could have thrown her hands up into the air, Elizabeth was certain she would have.

"I don't know," she said. "Honestly, I'm not sure why I didn't say anything. I think I'm . . . Well, I don't know how he'll react when he sees me. If he were to send me packing, I suppose I didn't want you or anyone else to know how ashamed I was." Elizabeth stared out toward the tree line, a dark smudge that was barely visible through the falling snow.

"Why would he do any such thing? I'd think he'd be happy to see you if he's any good brother at all."

"It's . . ." Elizabeth blinked away the traitorous tears that had gathered in the corners of her eyes. She'd pushed aside all her fear and doubts about Monroe as thoughts of Landon had taken over. But now that she was here with Penny, and had to explain it all again, they rushed back as if they'd never been gone at all. "I made a foolish mistake when I was younger. He did everything for me after our father died, and I repaid him by running off to marry a cowboy who wanted to become a miner. I didn't even tell him, Penny. He was my brother, and he loved me more than anything, and I . . . left him with a note. I never even wrote to him over seven years. I'm sure he thinks I hate him. If he doesn't believe me dead."

"Elizabeth." Penny laid a gloved hand on her arm. "If it's been that long, I'm sure all he'll be is happy to see you."

Elizabeth wanted to believe that, so badly, but she didn't dare hope. She'd been so horrible to him that God might only see it as right to punish her in return. He certainly had during all those years she'd lived in California. But she nodded, and that seemed to satisfy Penny.

"Perhaps today's train will arrive as usual, with Ben, your brother, and Emma on it," Penny said. "After all, I can't marry that tree in the lobby."

Elizabeth giggled. It was exactly what she needed. As she laughed with Penny, some of the fear melted away.

It even made it possible to think that Landon might answer her questions. After all, he wouldn't keep buying her ornaments and cutting down trees and *looking* at her the way he did last night if he didn't also see something between them.

Elizabeth's heart warmed even as her face froze in the snow. "Come on," she said to Penny. "Let's get inside and see if the kitchen has any coffee ready."

She looped arms with her new friend. The world seemed somehow brighter and more hopeful, even as the snow swirled furiously around them.

NOON CAME AND WENT without the train from Cañon City arriving. With only hotel guests to feed, both the girls at the lunch counter and in the dining room finished the meal service far more quickly than usual.

When Elizabeth entered the lobby with Genia, she found Penny wandering like a fretting ghost with Dora, Adelaide, and a redheaded girl—Millie, Elizabeth remembered. Elizabeth had tried to keep her own fears at bay since early that morning. The train probably hadn't left the station in Cañon City. Her brother and his wife were likely comfortable in a hotel there. And as much as she wished to see him again—and finally put her fears to rest—her heart broke for Penny, who was without her fiancé.

"We can always delay the weddings," Dora was saying when Elizabeth and Genia approached them.

"But that's not fair to you and Mr. Gilbert. Think of all our plans! I wouldn't postpone your wedding." Penny twisted her hands together as she glanced out the window. The wind and the snow had only increased in ferocity since early that morning. "I'm afraid for him. What if the train is stuck?"

The thought had crossed Elizabeth's mind, but she'd batted it away like a fly over a summer meal. "They wouldn't have left if the conductor saw a storm coming, would they?" she asked.

"I doubt it," Millie said. "But Mr. McFarland informed Penny that a couple of men volunteered to ride up the tracks a ways to ensure all is well." She turned to Penny. "If he's out there, they'll find him."

Penny didn't answer, and Elizabeth knew why. Riding out in this growing storm was danger in itself. Those men couldn't go too far, or they'd risk getting lost or stuck themselves if the storm worsened.

"There's nothing to do now but wait," Adelaide said. A small smile crossed her face. "Although I'm surprised my brother didn't fight off this storm singlehandedly. He's never been one for patience." When she saw Elizabeth's confused look, she added, "Penny's fiancé is my brother."

Elizabeth's heart warmed to the girl. Adelaide had shown her such kindness when Elizabeth had entered the hotel, desperate and alone. And now she also worried for a brother. Elizabeth reached for her hand. "I imagine he's trading stories with Mr. Hartley about pesky little sisters."

Adelaide gave her a grateful smile, even as Dora, Millie, and Genia traded confused looks.

Elizabeth wished there was something she could do to help them all take their minds from the situation. As she surveyed the lobby, her eyes landed on the proud but unadorned pine Landon had set up. "We should decorate the tree!"

One by one, the other girls nodded, and Dora even smiled. But Penny shook her head.

"Come on, Penny," Elizabeth said. "It will be good for you to do something. Besides, the candles we place on the tree will shine through the window. It will act as a beacon. Maybe it will help draw those we love toward us." It wasn't as if Penny's Sheriff Young or Monroe would be out there, wandering in the snow—or so Elizabeth prayed—but it could act as a symbol of their hope. "Maybe God will see it and answer our prayers."

She took Penny's hand and drew her toward the tree. Penny looked the green branches up and down. "All right, if we must, I suppose I'll help."

Elizabeth smiled. "I have some golden balls we can place on the tree. We must find candles and some more ribbon. Perhaps Chef will give us some of his dried fruit."

"I have a few striped peppermint candy canes I bought from the mercantile for gifts," Genia said.

"We could pop corn and put it on strings!" Adelaide said.

"I could make folded paper decorations if Mrs. McFarland will spare some paper," Dora added.

"I saw that once in a book," another girl named Edie chimed in. She had just joined them with a couple of the other waitresses. Her eyes were bright behind the wire-framed spectacles she wore, making it hard for Elizabeth to believe what she'd heard the other girls say about Edie—that a nefarious man had coerced her into stealing from the hotel, and she was slowly earning her way back into the company's good graces.

The girls mentioned more ideas, and Elizabeth grinned. This was exactly what she'd hoped would happen. As her new friends dispersed, she tasked herself with finding something that would be fitting for the very top of the tree. The kitchen seemed a likely place to start.

Elizabeth had taken only a few steps when Landon appeared. He looked different, and Elizabeth furrowed her brow, trying to figure out how. And then she saw it.

He was smiling.

Chapter Sixteen

"Good afternoon, Landon," Elizabeth said, his name rolling off her tongue as if she'd been saying it her entire life.

He tried not to show how much it meant to hear her say his name with such affection. His fingers dug into the gift he held for her behind his back. "Good afternoon," he said, more stiffly than he'd wanted.

That only made her smile more. It was as if she could see how awkward he felt.

Landon cleared his throat. "I'm sorry about last night. I shouldn't have left so abruptly. Were you in any trouble?"

"No. Mrs. Ruby only wanted to ensure I wasn't hurt. Although she did insist I find my way to my room before curfew from now on. But thank you for the apology. You do have a tendency to disappear."

Her words cut through him. But she was right. If a situation looked bad, he didn't stay around, and that wasn't fair to her—or gentlemanly in the least.

Elizabeth leaned a little to the left. "What are you hiding behind your back?"

He'd almost forgotten. He held out the star, and she gasped.

"This was just what I was looking for! Although I thought I might need to make something myself. How did you know?" She took the shining tin from his hands and held it before her, joy radiating from every part of her, an angel from head to toe.

"I realized you'd need something to place on the top of the tree. The woman at the store had ordered one some time ago, thinking the hotel might have a tree this year."

"It's perfect." She bestowed a smile upon him, so bright that he'd give her the stars in the sky to put on that fool tree too, if it would keep her smiling at him like that forever. And he hoped she would, even after he told her he needed to leave.

"I'll place it on the tree for you, if you like."

Elizabeth nodded, and he left to retrieve a ladder. When he returned, a few guests had gathered around the tree as a couple of the girls began to drape more of the red velvet ribbon from its branches. Two other girls sat before the fireplace, folding paper into intricate designs. And there was Elizabeth, beaming at the tree, her tin star clutched in her hands as the snow fell faster outside the window behind her.

That snow made him uneasy, but he pushed that feeling aside as he set up the ladder. Elizabeth handed him the star. He climbed to the top of the tree and set it on the topmost branch. The star caught the meager light from the window, and a sudden memory whirled back at Landon. He was young, maybe about seven or eight, and the owner of the ranch where his mother worked had let him place the star on top of the small tree that sat on a table. His little chest had swelled with pride at such an important job, and even though he knew they weren't related, he felt as if he was part of a large, loving family.

Looking at that star now, he had the strangest feeling that he was among family again. It made no sense. After all, he barely knew these people at the hotel, except Elizabeth. It felt as if he'd known her forever, even though it had only been six days. Yet still, as he looked down to her smiling face and the other girls and the guests watching him, a sense of warmth and belonging enveloped him.

Leaving was the last thing he wanted to do.

That thought almost made him topple from the ladder. He'd already been dreading what awaited him in Cañon City, and staying at the hotel had felt like hiding, like cowardice. But now it felt . . . different. He didn't want to leave because he liked it here.

"It looks perfect," Elizabeth said when he returned to the bottom of the ladder. "Thank you."

Her words might as well have been her arms, wrapping around him. She was so trusting. It amazed him. For a woman who had been married to a man who didn't seem to have been the best sort of husband, she still seemed to believe the world was full of wonder and hope.

It made him wonder if there was a different way . . .

Elizabeth was at the window now, peering into the white world beyond it. The snow swirled outside, obscuring the view completely. "I fear for those men who rode out to find the train."

Landon silently agreed, but didn't wish to worry her further. "They wouldn't have volunteered unless they knew what they were doing. I'm certain they'll be fine."

"What if they don't find the train? Or worse, what if they find it and . . ." She turned to him with big eyes, worry reflecting in them. "My brother is likely on that train, with his wife."

He wanted so badly to reach for her hand to reassure her. But that was impossible in this big room filled with people. So instead, he gave her a small smile and said, "They will be fine. The most likely scenario is that the train is moving slowly." He didn't add that Mr. McFarland had told him he'd telegraphed the station in Cañon City and learned the train left on time this morning and hadn't returned. "It may be on its way now. And if it isn't, the men searching for it will find it."

Her eyes traced his face as some of the worry lifted from her own. "Do you really believe that?"

"I do."

She smiled at him. "I trust you."

He wanted, so badly, to tell her. To let her know what he was planning. But she'd try to talk him out of it, and then where would he be? An even poorer cowboy who'd spent all his money staying in a hotel because he couldn't make up his mind. How could he ask for her then, with no way to provide for her? He couldn't. And so he swallowed the words that wanted to come out of his mouth.

He'd go to Cañon City and do what needed to be done. Then he'd return to this hotel as a rich man. Only then would he tell Elizabeth how he felt about her—when he would finally be in a place to deserve such feelings in return.

Then afterward, he'd steel his heart so the guilt at what he'd done and the secret he'd need to keep from Elizabeth wouldn't tear him apart. She watched him now, wisps of hair falling in graceful waves around her face. Those eyes held all the trust in the world, but she frowned just slightly, as if she realized that perhaps she wouldn't be wise to place that much trust in him.

She at least deserved to know he was still planning to leave town. He'd ask her to wait for him, if he could gather the courage. "Elizabeth—"

The front doors to the hotel slammed open, snow and wind howling their way into the lobby. The tree's branches shook. The bellboys struggled to get the doors shut again, and once they were, three frozen figures, covered in snow from head to toe, stood just inside.

Chapter Seventeen

"They're the men who went looking for the train!" Adelaide exclaimed from somewhere behind Elizabeth.

They were entirely covered in snow and looked frozen, but it was them. Elizabeth's heart beat faster. Maybe they'd found it! She said a quick prayer for good news and then glanced at Landon. He was watching her, looking as if he wanted to say something. But instead, he gestured toward the men.

Elizabeth shot him a smile just as Penny grabbed her arm.

"Oh, I hope they found it!" Penny said, Adelaide at her side. Together, the three of them joined the small crowd that had gathered around the men.

"Give them some room!" Mrs. McFarland hustled in and began helping the men unwrap from scarves and coats and hats.

"We found the train," one of them said, as soon as his face was free of his snow-encrusted scarf.

The questions began immediately.

"Where is it?" one of the guests asked.

"How are the passengers?" another said.

"Did you speak with anyone on the train?" Penny piped up. Elizabeth gripped her hand harder. Monroe had to be all right. She couldn't accept that he wasn't.

"Shh." Mrs. McFarland held a hand up from the pile of winter clothing in her arms. "Let the man speak."

One of the maids pushed through the crowd with an armload of blankets. The men took them and wrapped them around themselves before easing their way toward the nearest fireplace. Finally, the one man spoke again. "It's about five miles north of here. Some of the cars are derailed from the ice."

Penny gasped.

Elizabeth felt sick. What if the people inside had been hurt? She'd heard stories of derailed trains catching fire from the contents of the cars' stoves spilling out into the cars.

A panicked murmur rose in the crowd.

"The passengers seem fine," the man said, louder so as to be heard. "The derailment isn't so bad that anything caught fire. But they'll soon run out of coal to burn for warmth. We need to get them off that train as soon as we can," the man said as he took a steaming mug of tea that Mrs. Ruby handed him. "Thank you, ma'am."

"But we can't go out in this," a man in the crowd said. "They can use the coal meant for the locomotive."

"The storm has worsened," one of the other searchers said. "And the train was due to be coaled once it arrived here. There isn't enough of it onboard. These people have but maybe a few hours. We can't leave them out there. As soon as I'm warmed through, I'll lead us back out there. If we stay on the tracks, we won't be lost."

The other searchers agreed, and slowly, one by one, men in the crowd volunteered to go with them.

"I'll go," a deep, clipped voice said from behind Elizabeth.

Landon. She turned, and he nodded at her. She wanted to throw her arms around him and beg him to bring her brother and his wife back. But all she did was nod gratefully.

The crowd broke up as the men who agreed to rescue the passengers from the train went to bundle up for the journey.

"We should prepare rooms for them," Dora said from where she lingered nearby. "Stoke up the fires, ensure there are plenty of blankets, and be ready to help any who might have injuries."

The other girls nodded, and Mrs. Ruby directed them to help the maids prepare empty rooms for the passengers.

"Come, help," Dora said to Penny, who still stood attached to Elizabeth's arm in a daze. "Working will busy your mind. Then he'll be here before you know it."

Penny nodded slowly. "You're right."

"I'll be there in a moment," Elizabeth said. As soon as the girls were gone, she turned to where Landon had been standing before. He was gone now, likely up to his room to gather his coat and other necessities.

Elizabeth raced up the stairs as fast as propriety would let her, although she doubted anyone was watching or cared at this moment. The entire hotel was in a tizzy. Just as she turned the corner to the south wing hallway, she found him. He wore that same long coat, but also carried his hat, a scarf, thick gloves, and two wool blankets.

"Thank you," she said. "I had to find you and tell you that before you left."

"I can't stand by and let people freeze to death," he said, placing the hat on his head. It sat at a slightly rakish angle, and Elizabeth wondered if that was how he wore it when he was out driving cattle. The mere image of it made her swallow hard.

"I'll bring your brother back," he said.

Tears stung her eyes, but Elizabeth forced them away. She wouldn't dwell on bad possibilities; only good. So instead of mourning, she gave Landon a description of her brother as best she could remember him. "I don't know what his wife looks like, but she should be with him." She twisted her hands together as the worry she fought so hard to keep at bay tried to claw its way out.

Landon set down the items in his arms, took her hands, and gently pried them apart. "I told you I'd bring your brother back. Do you trust me?"

She dragged her eyes from his calloused hands that held hers so tightly and yet so softly, up to those eyes that seemed to know her very soul. "I do," she said, barely audible.

"You have my word." He stood there a moment, not saying anything but holding her gaze.

If she was braver—if she didn't carry the baggage of a long and trying marriage—Elizabeth would yank her hands from his and use them to pull his face closer. Instead, she just stood there while he held her hands, her eyes, and her heart.

He laced his fingers through hers and she thought she could stand in this one place forever, so long as he kept holding her like this and looking at her as if his life depended on her very existence.

"Thank you again for going," she said. "Please be safe."

"I will. The sooner we can rescue those folks, the sooner the train can get back on its rails, and the sooner I can get to Cañon City." He smiled at her and rubbed his thumbs on the backs of her hands before letting go. "And now I must go." He tugged at the brim of his hat and leaned over to pick up the blankets, scarf, and gloves. And then he winked at her and was off, around the corner to the stairs.

Elizabeth leaned against the smooth wooden wall, barely able to understand what had just happened.

He was still planning to take that job.

It didn't matter how he felt about her—or she about him. He'd taken her for granted. Led her along like a calf on a rope, only to leave her here while he went to do something he despised even though he'd be back to ranch work again as soon as the snow began to melt. He wouldn't return to the hotel.

One thing was clear: she cared more for him than he did for her.

Chapter Eighteen

The wind snapped the ends of Landon's blanket against his coat. He had to duck his head against the snow or risk it stinging the parts of his face that were still left bare. He could barely see the horse in front of him as the rescue group rode single file down the railroad tracks. Five miles was beginning to feel more like five hundred miles.

At least it was easy to tell they were still on the tracks. When Ulysses veered sideways, his hoofs would strike the metal rails. They couldn't be too far away now. He promised Elizabeth he'd bring back her brother and his wife, and he'd do it, even if he froze to death in the process.

To keep warm, he imagined the look on her face when he returned. First, her big, beautiful eyes would light up in surprise. She'd clap her hand to her mouth and run to him, ignoring anyone who might be watching. She'd fling her arms around him and press her lips to his and tell him how grateful she was that he was here.

Of course, to imagine that, he had to ignore that strange, closed-off look she gave him right before he left. It didn't last long, and it was barely noticeable, but her hands had gone stiff, and her smile had disappeared. It had to be fear. Nothing else made sense. She was already afraid for her brother, and now she feared him going out in this storm. Once he returned, she'd be her usual radiant self.

A howling gust of wind threatened to tear the outermost blanket from him. He grabbed hold of it and yanked it to him, holding the ends together with one hand and the reins with the other. Next winter, he'd be warm in his own home on his own land. He'd watch blizzards like this from behind windows that overlooked acres that he owned. And if he dared hope hard enough, Elizabeth would be there with him.

The thought made him both happy and terrified. If she agreed to marry him, and she found out later how he'd gotten the money for his own spread, she would never forgive him. Did he even deserve her if he couldn't be honest with her? Perhaps Aimee had been right. Maybe he didn't deserve a good woman—whether he was a poor cowboy or a rancher who'd bought his cattle with stolen money.

The doubt gnawed away at him as they rode farther north. It was still there, freezing him from the inside out when the stopped train finally came into view.

"Stay close to the cars if you ride down!" the man in the lead shouted over the wind as the line of riders split up to go from car to car. "Bring the extra horses up here!"

Landon pushed Ulysses ahead. He needed to find Monroe Hartley. He dismounted at the first car, tying off his horse as fast as possible. Inside, the passengers huddled around the stove in the middle of the car.

"Oh, thank goodness!" a woman said when she saw him.

This was clearly a first-class car, with the passengers dressed warmly in fine coats and hats. A few of the other riders entered behind him and began escorting the passengers to the waiting horses.

"Monroe Hartley?" Landon called out. No one responded. As Landon entered the second car and the third, with no Mr. Hartley in either of those cars either, he began to realize this rescue mission would need more than one trip back and forth to the hotel. There were simply too many passengers and not enough horses.

In the fourth car, the scene was much like the first, with passengers crowded around a warm stove. Landon called again for Elizabeth's brother, but this time, someone answered.

"I'm Hartley." A dark-haired man moved out from where he stood behind a woman who was wrapped head to toe in a coat and blankets.

If he'd been the sort, Landon would have dropped down on his knees and thanked God right there in the train car. Instead, he whispered a quick prayer of thanks under his breath and reached out to shake Hartley's hand. "Someone asked me specifically to look for you and your wife."

Hartley wrinkled his forehead. "Might I ask who?"

Landon shook his head. It wasn't his place to insert himself into Elizabeth's reunion with her brother. Instead, he said simply, "I don't know her."

"It must be Penny or Dora," the woman who'd been crouching in front of him said. She rose to take his arm, and Landon presumed this was Hartley's wife. "They have to be worried about us, especially after so many delays."

"We have horses outside, but not many. If you come with me, I'll ensure you both arrive at the hotel safely." Landon stepped back to allow the couple to go before him.

But Hartley shook his head. "Take my wife to the hotel, please, and these other ladies and the children first. I'll wait."

"I don't want to leave you," his wife said, turning toward him.

Landon averted his eyes to the other passengers, not wanting to intrude on a private moment. He did admire the man's honor, though. He would've done the same if he'd been in this position.

"I'll be fine. You go. You need to take care of yourself, remember?" Hartley said.

She didn't respond, and Landon snuck a glance back to them. Hartley embraced his wife and then let go. "Go on," he said. Then he looked up at Landon. "You'll see her safely there?"

"You have my word." With a nod of his head, he guided Mrs. Hartley, four other women, and two small children toward the front of the car.

Outside, the storm hadn't calmed at all. One at a time, he led each woman—and carried both children—to the last remaining horses.

"I have one more child!" one of the men shouted from the first car. "Is there any room?"

"I'll take him," Landon said, tapping Ulysses into motion. He rode alongside the car, and the man placed the young boy in front of Landon.

The boy shivered as he waved to a woman standing in the doorway to the car. Landon wrapped one of the blankets around him.

"Is that your mama?" Landon asked.

The boy nodded, tears beginning to drip down his cheeks.

"I'm Mr. Cooper. What's your name?"

"William."

"Well, William, I'm personally going to make sure your mama gets to the hotel as soon as possible, all right?"

"All right," the boy said hesitantly. He must have been no more than five or six. Landon's heart ached for him. The sooner they got back to the hotel, the sooner he could return for both this boy's mother and Elizabeth's brother. He rode back to where Hartley's wife sat waiting on a horse with another woman.

"Let's go!" the man in the lead shouted over the storm.

Slowly, the line of rescuers and passengers moved forward, into the blizzard. Landon looked back at the train, but it quickly disappeared into the snow.

He'd heard the passengers say they'd already taken most of the extra coal meant to be used by the engine. They needed to move quickly and return before the remaining passengers ran out of heat. But as the wind blew even harder, and the snow fell faster, doubts crept into Landon's mind.

They'd be lucky if the group of them even made it back to the hotel without freezing first.

Chapter Nineteen

Elizabeth paced the distance between the fireplaces. Again. And again. And again. It had been hours since the rescuers had left

"Stop." A gentle hand grabbed hold of her arm. It was Dora.

"I'm sorry. I can't seem to remain still when we don't know what's happening out there." Elizabeth waved her free hand at the hotel doors.

Dora let go, but she didn't move. "Penny told me about your brother."

Elizabeth stole a glance at Penny, whose eyes hadn't left the window and whose hands hadn't stopped worrying the fabric of her dress. She should be upset with Penny for betraying her confidence, but she wasn't. Not when she couldn't even remember why she'd kept the secret to begin with.

"But it's something else, isn't it?" Dora asked.

Elizabeth drew in a breath. Dora watched her with quiet, nonjudgmental eyes. Elizabeth had grown so used to being on her own. Although she'd befriended the handful of miners' wives in the camp, those friendships never lasted long. The women often grew tired of the rough and dirty camp, and left to return home to await their husbands. Or the men simply gave up, and the family would leave the camp. It had been years since Elizabeth had other women she could truly confide in.

And if anyone could understand her predicament, it was these women—Penny and Dora, and Caroline at the store—who had risked their jobs, their reputations, and their hearts for the men they loved.

"It is," Elizabeth said quietly.

Dora gave her a knowing smile. "It's easy to see if one knows what she's looking for."

"What do you mean?"

"The way you and Mr. Cooper care for each other. You're worried for him out there, aren't you?"

Elizabeth sighed, scared to admit it out loud, but also relieved to share her fear with someone else. "I am. Although I shouldn't be, I'm so afraid for him."

"You can't deny your heart. I know that well enough." Dora led Elizabeth to a nearby chair. Although hotel employees weren't normally allowed to sit in guest areas, the blizzard seemed to blur the lines of propriety. No one had said anything, and even Mrs. Ruby sat in a wing chair near the fire, deep in conversation with Mrs. McFarland.

"That isn't it." Elizabeth glanced out the window. The snow was relentless. She tried not to think about it, but it was hard to ignore the danger everyone out there faced.

Dora tilted her head. "Then what's troubling you? Besides the storm."

Elizabeth closed her eyes. He'd said those words so loosely, almost as if they didn't matter. Almost as if they didn't break her heart upon their impact. "He's leaving."

Dora said nothing. Instead, she reached for Elizabeth's hand and just held it, letting her know she was there to listen.

"He has work waiting for him in Cañon City. But he said it wasn't anything he cared to do. His regular work will be available again in spring. The longer he remained here, the more I believed he'd decided not to take on that other job. I thought, perhaps, he stayed here because of me. I've been so foolish." She shook her head. She wouldn't cry. She hadn't in years, and she wouldn't now. Not in the hotel lobby in front of everyone.

"Perhaps he means to return after he finishes his work?" Dora said.

"But wouldn't he have said as much? Why would he tell me he was leaving, then give me a smile, and go? He had to know what he was doing. He was letting me down, telling me that what we have isn't . . . isn't what I thought it was." Her voice broke on the last word, and Elizabeth clamped her mouth shut.

"I don't know," Dora said. "Men are strange with their words at times. They don't say things they should, and say things they shouldn't."

"He had to know what he was saying." Elizabeth turned her gaze to the window again. "He never says much, but what he does say always matters. If he intended to return, he would have told me."

Dora squeezed her hand. "He'll be back here soon with the passengers. Maybe you can speak with him then?"

Elizabeth shook her head. She wouldn't seek him out. She'd already embarrassed herself enough, falling for yet another heartless cowboy. She'd been nothing but a passing entertainment for him. And the sooner she came to terms with that, the better off she would be. At least he was honorable enough to help find her brother. "I have my work here. I hope I'm proving to Mrs. Ruby that I'm worthy of becoming a Gilbert Girl."

"Oh, I have no doubt about that. Mrs. Ruby has praised your initiative more than once. And you've caught on quickly at the lunch counter. Before you know it, you'll have a contract and a place in the dining room," Dora said.

A knock sounded at the door, and the entire room went still for a solid second before it burst into motion again. Both Elizabeth and Dora jumped up.

"It's the passengers!" someone shouted.

"Quick, girls!" Mrs. Ruby leapt up faster than Elizabeth had thought she was capable. "Help the maids get these people to their rooms, and then come to the kitchen to fetch them some soup."

Elizabeth remained planted in place as the other girls moved forward. She held a hand to her mouth as she searched the people streaming inside from the storm. He had to be there. He simply had to.

She didn't even know which *he* she was hoping to see as she scanned the faces. They were all women, and some children, except for the riders who'd gone to find them.

"Is that everyone?" Mr. McFarland asked.

"No. There are still some women and all of the men onboard. We need to go out again," a man said, his face bright red from the cold.

"I'll go with you. The hotel can watch itself." Mr. McFarland disappeared, as his wife trailed after him, begging him to dress appropriately for the storm.

Beside her, Penny slumped into a chair. "He isn't there."

"Of course he isn't," Adelaide said. "Didn't you hear the man?"

"I know." Penny shut her eyes. "I just hoped . . ."

Elizabeth had hoped too. She scanned the faces one more time until her eyes landed on Landon in the very back. He was wrapped in a coat and blanket and carried a child who appeared to be asleep in his arms.

"Landon!" she said without thinking. She ran forward, ignoring the sensible part of herself that promised not to seek him out again. She didn't intend to ask him about his feelings for her or his future plans; she wanted only to know if he'd seen her brother or Sheriff Young. And to find out why he was carrying a child.

"Elizabeth. Follow me." He led the way down the north wing hall, and Elizabeth rushed to keep up with him. One of the maids ushered them into a room. She pulled down the bedcovers as Landon set the boy on a chair. "He needs to get these wet clothes off. Make him as warm as possible. He passed out about halfway here. I'm afraid . . ." He didn't finish the sentence, and he didn't need to.

Elizabeth jumped into action, helping the maid peel off the boy's snow-soaked coat and clothing. She wrapped him in a towel and laid him on the bed. "Do we have any hot irons?"

The maid nodded and ran from the room.

Briefly, Elizabeth realized she was breaking the cardinal rule in the hotel by being alone with Landon, but surely no one cared right now. Besides, this little boy was here too. Not to mention she had no intention of letting Landon get close to her again. He'd already made his plans quite clear, and Elizabeth refused to be taken for a fool again.

"His name is William," Landon said. He reached out and put a hand on the little boy's arm.

Elizabeth's heart ached. "We'll do everything we can. I promise."

Landon stood for a moment, quiet, with his hand resting on William's arm. "I know you will," he finally said, shrugging off the blanket.

Elizabeth tilted her head. Landon's face was still red, and now perspiration dotted his brow. "Are you feeling well?"

"I'm fine. I need to go back for his mama. And for your brother." He swiped an arm across his forehead.

Elizabeth grabbed on to the side of the bed where she sat. "You saw him?"

Landon turned to look at her. She knew she should look away. She was doing her heart no favors by allowing herself to be drawn into his gaze again.

Yet she didn't move.

"I did," he said. "He insisted I bring his wife. I'll find out where they've placed her."

Elizabeth nodded. "Thank you." She turned back to the boy. She could hear Landon's footsteps leaving the room. How could a man who was so gentle with a child be so cruel when it came to her heart? Nothing about his actions made any sense.

As she watched William, asleep in the chair, she thought more about this job of Landon's. Yes, he'd made it clear it was something he didn't care to do, and yet he felt as if he needed to. But nothing about that indicated why he'd leave and not return. Nothing fit with the way he'd seemingly toyed with her emotions. He didn't seem the sort of man to go out of his way to do that kind of thing.

Part of her wondered if there was something else. Something he hadn't told her. But she knew that was only wishful thinking. He might have seemed more sincere than Colin, but underneath, he was the same.

She sighed and stood just as the maid returned with the hot irons. Elizabeth helped her wrap them in the bedclothes so they'd warm, but not burn, the little boy. Then she went to hunt down some dry clothing that might fit him. And she forced herself not to think any more on Landon.

Chapter Twenty

The ride back out to the train took longer than either of the two previous rides. The horses moved slower and the men seemed less inclined to hurry them along. It was a dangerous path of thinking, Landon knew. And yet, he could do nothing from his place in the middle of the line.

By the time they reached the train, it was dusk. The temperatures had already begun to dip lower and the snow continued to fall. And yet Landon felt uncomfortably warm. The cold was likely getting to his head.

"We have to move faster," Landon said to McFarland as they jumped down from their horses. "Else we'll all freeze out here."

"I'll speak to the men and lead on the return," McFarland said. "Will you take the rear to ensure no one falls behind?"

Landon nodded before swinging himself inside the first car. Men streamed toward the door. It seemed most of the remaining passengers had congregated in the first and second cars. After ensuring Hartley that his wife had made it safely to the hotel and William's mother of the same, he proceeded through each car, checking for stragglers. In a way, this wasn't unlike driving cattle.

Sometimes he thought he might miss those drives, but missing them was pointless. Rumors were already rampant that the Colorado & New Mexico Railway would run cars specifically for cattle down these lines, eliminating the need for men to drive them to Cañon City. He could continue, work as a ranch hand, of course, but the thought of doing that on another man's ranch for the rest of his life wasn't something Landon could stomach.

No, his decision to obtain money to buy land fast was his best option, even if his method of doing so wasn't entirely legal. Or honorable. Or something he would ever feel comfortable doing.

Satisfied the cars were empty, Landon returned to the front. A wave of heat washed over him, almost buckling his knees. He grabbed hold of one of the seats in the car as black dots danced in front of his eyes. They cleared, leaving a feeling of dread in his stomach. He shook his head to try to chase away the feeling. He was cold and exhausted, that was all. Once they got these people back to the hotel, he'd rest.

Most of the passengers were on horses now. Two women sat astride a horse, one without a coat. It was William's mother, and she was already shivering.

"Here." Landon shrugged out of his own coat and placed it around her shoulders, ignoring the cold that instantly bit through his shirt sleeves.

"No, you shouldn't," she said. "You'll freeze."

"I have a blanket. And you have a child who needs looking after."

"Thank you," she said, a grateful smile crossing her lips, which hadn't stopped chattering.

Landon returned to his horse and wrapped the wool blanket around himself. He'd forgotten to retrieve the second blanket from William. This one wasn't as warm as his coat, but if they made good time, he'd be fine.

The line lurched forward, and Landon hung back. He nodded at Hartley to go in front of him, and then he fell in, leaving the empty train behind.

They plodded through the snow. Minutes passed. Landon lost track of time. His mind wandered, from the little boy to Elizabeth to cattle rustling to the cold that enveloped him. Oddly, even though it grew darker and the wind and snow didn't let up, he began to feel warmer. Hot, almost. His head pounded, and it became hard to keep his eyes open.

He shrugged the blanket off, letting it fall. He couldn't fall asleep. He needed to watch for people lagging behind. But after some time, he could no longer fight it. His eyes drifted closed, and a smile crossed his face as he imagined Elizabeth taking his hand and leading him into the hotel.

Chapter Twenty-one

Elizabeth sat with William for an hour. The color slowly came back to his cheeks, and he'd even moaned and turned over a couple of times.

"That's a good sign," the maid said. She'd been there the entire time, too, and Elizabeth had learned her name was Helen. She was a small, young wisp of a girl, but Elizabeth could tell none of that had any bearing on her capability.

The little boy's eyes fluttered open and looked at each of them. "Mama?"

"Shh." Elizabeth caressed his cheek. "Your mama will be here soon. Do you remember the man who rescued you from the train?"

"Mr. Cooper." The boy smiled. "He was nice. He's a cowboy."

Elizabeth couldn't help but grin back at him. Landon had certainly made an impression on this boy. "Mr. Cooper has gone back for your mother. She'll be here before you know it."

The boy nodded, seemingly satisfied. Helen offered him some soup. He sat up and eyed the bowl.

Now that the boy was awake and alert, Elizabeth stood. "I'll return in just a moment," she said. "I must go see to another passenger from the train."

William was too intent on his soup to answer, but Helen smiled. "We'll be fine here. Go on."

Elizabeth slipped out the door, taking a moment to stretch her back. It ached from sitting on the side of the bed, watching little William. Seeing him helpless as he'd been earlier, she was almost glad his mother wasn't here to see him like that. She couldn't imagine how heart-wrenching that would be. And yet . . .

It made Elizabeth remember how badly she'd wanted children. It was a desire she'd buried soon after she and Colin had arrived in California. And not too long after that, she'd found herself on her knees nearly every night, praying *not* to have children. God had granted her prayers, but now she wondered if she might have the opportunity again, someday.

The thought returned Landon to her mind, and she winced. She'd expected too much of him. The truth hurt, but at least she was no longer acting the fool.

She made her way upstairs, where Landon had informed her Monroe's wife had been placed in a room. She arrived to find a woman huddled in a blanket and sitting in a chair near the fireplace, a bowl of soup forgotten on the desk. Dora hovered nearby.

"Mrs. Hartley?" Elizabeth said hesitantly. It felt strange to use her own maiden name to address this woman she'd never met.

Her brother's wife turned slowly to look at Elizabeth. Her face was pale and surrounded with dark hair that had been recently brushed and plaited. But her green eyes were dull, and even when she smiled, it looked hollow.

"Yes?" she said.

Dora looked between the two of them. "I'll be back shortly." She gave the woman a hug. "I'm so happy you're back. We'll have more time to talk later."

Elizabeth entered the room as Dora left. She took her time closing the door behind her before turning to face Mrs. Hartley again. "We've not met, but Monroe may have mentioned me to you. I'm Elizabeth Campbell. Elizabeth Hartley Campbell." She remained near the door, her hands clasped before her.

Mrs. Hartley's face gave a spark of life. "You're Lizzie?"

Elizabeth nodded. Only Monroe had ever called her Lizzie. The nickname warmed her and yet made her want to crumple to the floor in shame.

"I don't believe it." Her brother's wife looked at her as if she were an apparition. "I'm sorry. I failed to introduce myself. I'm Emma Hartley, your brother's wife. Please call me Emma. After all, we're sisters now." Emma reached out a shaking hand, and Elizabeth took it gratefully. She pulled the desk chair over and sat next to Emma.

Emma's hand still shook as she returned it to her lap. Elizabeth eyed her new sister. She didn't look well at all.

"Are you feeling ill? Would you like to lie down?" she asked.

"No, but perhaps later. As soon as I know Monroe is here."

Elizabeth frowned. Emma didn't answer her first question. But she didn't feel she knew Emma well enough to press the subject. "He should be here soon," she said. It had been a couple of hours since the men had left again. It was dark now, and growing later. And colder. Elizabeth didn't want to think too much on that. They would be back. Landon had promised her. Even if she couldn't trust him with her heart, she knew he wouldn't break that promise.

"I hope so. I'm worried, Lizzie. Is it all right if I call you Lizzie, too?" Emma asked with the kindest smile.

"I suppose it is," Elizabeth replied, even as her face burned red. But beneath the shame of what she'd done to her brother were happier memories. Perhaps it wouldn't be so bad to be called Lizzie again. "Please don't worry. I know they'll get the rest of the passengers off the train and back here safely."

"I'll do my best." Emma gave her a grateful, if strained, smile.

They sat together for some time, talking and getting to know one another. Elizabeth asked again if Emma felt well, and the woman insisted she was fine. But as the hours dragged on, they both grew more restless.

"What could be keeping them?" Elizabeth wondered out loud.

"Do you suppose something has happened?" Emma clutched her blanket closer.

"No, of course not." *I hope.*

It was nearly midnight when Dora opened the door. "They've returned," she said quietly.

Elizabeth jumped up. Emma moved a little slower, and Dora rushed in to take her friend's arm. "Why don't you wait here? I'll find Mr. Hartley and send him to you."

"No, I'll go. He must be freezing." Emma moved toward the door.

Elizabeth forced herself to hold the door open for Dora and Emma, even though she was anxious to get to the lobby herself.

"Why don't you go ahead?" Dora suggested once they were in the hallway. "I'll walk with Emma."

"I'll find him," Elizabeth said, grateful to finally allay her fears. From the landing, she could see people below, the riders and the rescued both covered in snow. Two men held another person between them. And several of her new friends and other hotel employees were there, taking coats and blankets, offering hot drinks, and leading people to empty rooms. From above, Elizabeth couldn't tell one man from the next.

She ran down the stairs as quickly as possible. At the bottom, she pushed her way through the mass of people, scanning each face she saw. Many of the people who had returned, both passengers and riders alike, looked frozen to the bone. The word "frostbite" echoed in her ears as she passed. It shouldn't have come as a surprise considering how long these people had been outside, but it made her already racing heart beat even harder. What if they weren't all right? What if something had happened along the way? What if they weren't here at all?

She was just feet from the door when she finally spotted them. Two men—her brother and Mr. McFarland—held a third man between them. A snow-encrusted hat barely held on to the third man's head. He wore no coat and had no blanket wrapped about him. And he was unconscious.

"Landon," Elizabeth whispered. She stopped where she was, right in front of the trio.

"Lizzie?" Her brother's voice sounded incredulous in her ears. "Is that you? How...? What are you doing here?"

Elizabeth tore her eyes from Landon's slumped form. Monroe's face was bright red from the cold, and the dark hair that showed under his hat dripped melting snow onto his coat.

"I..." She didn't know what to say. After all this time, after all the different ways she'd imagined seeing her brother again, she had no words to speak.

"Mrs. Campbell is a waitress here at the hotel," Mr. McFarland filled in for her. He glanced back and forth between herself and Monroe. "Might I ask how you know each other?"

"She's my sister," Monroe said in a stunned voice.

Mr. McFarland raised his eyebrows but said nothing beyond, "Come, let's get Mr. Cooper to a room quickly. Mrs. Campbell, could you fetch some blankets and hot irons? If we don't warm him up soon, I fear he may not revive at all."

Elizabeth clutched her hands to her stomach, her attention once again on Landon. His face was so white it was nearly blue, and yet his forehead shone with perspiration. It didn't make sense at all. "Where is his coat?"

"He gave it to a woman who didn't have one," Mr. McFarland replied. "It saved her life, but I fear it may cost him his own."

Elizabeth stared at Landon, as if just looking at him might make him wake up. What if he didn't? *Oh, dear God, please help him.* Even if he didn't care for her the way she did for him, he didn't deserve this.

"Room 117 is empty," one of the maids said from nearby.

That spurred Elizabeth into action. She would save Landon's life if it were the last thing she did. She refused to let him die.

Chapter Twenty-two

At first, Landon didn't know where he was. He opened his eyes expecting to see the sky or the beams of a bunkhouse. But instead, a whitewashed ceiling stared back at him.

The hotel. It came back to him in bits and pieces. Arriving here. He was supposed to be somewhere else. But he wasn't. It was important. But it flitted from his mind as the pain arrived.

His head pounded so hard he thought it might burst open. And the heat . . . it felt as if he were on fire.

And then an angel's face appeared above him.

"Landon?" she said.

He felt himself smile before his eyes closed again.

WHEN HE WOKE AGAIN, he didn't open his eyes right away. He waited a moment, but there was only a dull, lingering pain in the back of his head. Nothing like before. And the heat had diminished. He let his eyes open for a split second. It was nighttime, and Elizabeth sat nearby, watching the fireplace. Her hand rested on his arm, but she wasn't alone.

He closed his eyes as she spoke to someone else. Another woman, who said she'd return in a moment.

As soon as she was gone, he felt the pillows adjust under his head. This was nice. He could lie here forever, comfortable in this bed, with an angel watching over him.

"Monroe has come by more than once," she said.

He opened one eye just a slit. She wasn't looking at his face. Instead, she was adjusting his bedcovers. He wanted to speak, to let her know he was awake, but the words wouldn't come. His throat was scratchy, as if he'd swallowed cactus needles.

"He's asked about your fever. And about me. I should speak with him, I know I should, but I don't know what to say. Leaving him with barely a word was a mistake. Marrying Colin was the worst choice I've ever made. I suppose I was too embarrassed to write to Monroe after that. So I didn't . . . and that was wrong too."

Landon wanted to open his eyes, but now it felt too late. She must have thought he was asleep.

"I believe the only right thing I've done in my life is to come here. For the first time, I feel as if I have a future that might be good." She rested a hand on his arm. Landon didn't dare move.

"I was so upset with you when you left. But now . . . Maybe it's for the best. Maybe I need to be on my own for some time. You're a cowboy, and I've been through this before. I should've known better. I'll always care for you, though. I hope you know that."

Landon's heart constricted at her words. She didn't want him. She—how did she put it? She *cared for him.* What did that mean? Clearly it wasn't enough to want to make a life with him. He was just a cowboy to her. Someone too low to love. Someone who couldn't be trusted.

And she was right. After all, he'd been planning to build a life with her based on a lie.

She was better off without him. He turned over, pretending to still be asleep. The door opened, and another woman spoke to Elizabeth. She left, and he opened his eyes to stare at the wall.

As soon as he was well enough and the snow had stopped falling, he'd be gone.

Chapter Twenty-three

It had been two days since the passengers were rescued from the train. The snow had finally ended early the day before, and men had gone to dig out the tracks. They'd brought the re-railer from the depot, kept there in case of just such an emergency, and after several hours of work, had gotten the derailed cars back onto the tracks. The train had stopped by the hotel earlier in the day and picked up the passengers who were well enough and ready to finish their trip to Santa Fe.

It was nearing evening now on Christmas Eve, and Elizabeth had finally left Landon's side. He'd seemed more coherent today, although he still hadn't woken entirely. But the fever had broken, and Elizabeth knew she could no longer put off the inevitable.

She needed to speak with her brother.

She entered the lobby, uncertain where to find him. The spacious room bustled with activity, but one thing drew Elizabeth's eyes—the tree. It sparkled from top to bottom with lit candles. Ribbon cascaded down in curled lengths. Paper ornaments and chains of popped corn were draped around its boughs. And at the top, where Landon had placed it, the tin star sparkled in the candlelight.

It was absolutely beautiful.

"Do you like it?" Penny arrived at Elizabeth's side.

"I . . . I love it! When did you have time to do this?" Elizabeth couldn't take her eyes from the tree.

"The girls and I had plenty of time while you were keeping vigil by Mr. Cooper's side."

Elizabeth's face grew warm. How many other people had noticed how much time she'd spent with Landon? She hoped Mrs. Ruby saw it as simple Christian charity and nothing more. She hadn't asked Elizabeth to take her usual place in the lunch counter, and Genia had stopped by to inform her that Mrs. Ruby had excused her from her duties while she nursed Mr. Cooper.

She looked at Penny now. Her friend was smiling, more vibrant than she'd appeared in days. "How is Sheriff Young?"

"He's well. I'm just so happy he's here and we can be married." Penny's smile was as bright as the candles on the tree. "I've heard your Mr. Cooper is recovering nicely."

"He's stirred a few times, but hasn't awoken yet. Soon, I hope. If you'll forgive me, I must find my brother."

"The last I saw him, he was finishing dinner with Emma." Penny gestured at the dining room.

"Thank you. And thank you again for finishing the tree. It's lovely." Elizabeth gave her friend a smile before turning toward the dining room. The door opened just as she stepped forward, and a few guests emerged, including Monroe and Emma.

Elizabeth stopped, unsure again of how or even if she wanted to approach her brother. But Emma spotted her before she could turn and run back to Landon's room. Emma whispered something into Monroe's ear, and then walked off toward where Penny still stood near the tree.

"Lizzie?" Monroe said as he moved toward her. "It's good to see you about. How fares Mr. Cooper?"

"He's much improved, though not yet awake." Elizabeth was glad for the small talk, even if it did have to revolve around Landon. "He's lucky you found him." Dora had informed her that Monroe had been the one to spot Landon's horse walking behind him without a rider. He'd returned and found Landon, unconscious in the snow. "He's alive because of you."

Her brother shifted, seemingly uncomfortable with the praise. A short moment passed, and Elizabeth was finally able to observe how much he'd changed over the years. He was no longer the boy she'd known. Then again, she was no longer the girl he'd looked after. He gestured at the nearby seating. "Let's sit."

Elizabeth shook her head. "I couldn't. That is, I'm not supposed to."

Monroe placed his hands on the back of a very comfortable-looking wing chair. "I built this hotel, so I believe I get some degree of authority. And I say that after two straight days of nursing an ill man, you deserve to sit in this chair."

Elizabeth couldn't help but smile despite the sick feeling in her stomach. She sat, and hoped Mrs. Ruby or the McFarlands didn't just happen to walk by anytime soon.

Monroe sat across from her and leaned forward. He shook his head. "I'm still amazed you're here."

"I came to find you," Elizabeth said. She couldn't look at him, so she kept her eyes on her hands, which were clasped in her lap.

"After all these years . . . why? Honestly, I'd thought you dead. I mourned you, Lizzie."

She squeezed her eyes shut. She was a terrible person to have caused her own brother such pain.

"Will you at least tell me why? I deserve that much."

She took a deep breath. "Colin died."

"I'm sorry to hear that," Monroe said stiffly.

Elizabeth opened her eyes and glanced up at him. His mouth was set in a line, and his feelings about her former husband were evident in the hard set of his jaw. "I was not," she barely whispered.

He tilted his head, obviously confused.

"He was . . . Our marriage . . ." Several years' worth of tears that had been held back seemed to climb up Elizabeth's throat, and she pressed a hand to her mouth until the feeling passed. "It wasn't what I expected it to be," she said as fast as she could. She didn't trust herself not to break down completely. "He was angry and cruel and distant. He hated mining and he seemed to take it out on me."

"He hurt you?" Monroe's hands had balled into fists.

"Not physically," she said. "Never like that. But it was miserable."

He relaxed some, but not entirely. "I tried to tell you—"

"I know you did. And I'm sorry I didn't listen. Monroe, I'm so sorry for everything. I always meant to write you, not that it excuses the way I left. But when things turned out so badly, I couldn't bring myself to. What would I have said?"

"You could have told me how unhappy you were. I would've sent you train fare to return to the ranch." He closed his eyes briefly before opening them again to look at her. "We waited for you, Colette and I. For nearly a year. I was afraid you'd write and I wouldn't be there to receive your letter. We didn't leave until it finally became obvious you weren't going to write. I had no way of knowing where you were, no way to search for you. Can you imagine how that felt?"

Elizabeth nodded. She bit down hard on her lip to keep the emotions that rolled through her at bay. "Monroe, I'm so sorry. I don't know what else to say. I was wrong and there is no way for me to make that up to you now."

He said nothing, not right away, and Elizabeth decided to ask a question that had been on her mind. "What happened with Colette?"

Monroe folded his hands together. "She died, about two and a half years ago now. It nearly killed me too. Then I met Emma."

"I'm so sorry," Elizabeth said. "I should have been there."

He sat back in the chair, silent again. After a moment, he gestured at the tree. "I've been told you decorated this entire hotel for Christmas."

She smiled a bit as she thought of Landon cutting down that tree and the girls helping her make decorations. "I didn't do it alone."

Monroe's eyes drifted back to her. "I'm sure you made him a fine wife, Lizzie. It isn't your fault he was a terrible husband."

They were exactly the words she needed to hear. And now there was no holding it back. It was as if a dam had burst under a raging river. The tears started to fall, one by one. Elizabeth hid her face in her hands, unable, for the first time in seven years, to stop it from happening.

Comforting arms wrapped around her. Her brother. The only family she had left.

"I'm so happy to see you," he said. "This was the best Christmas gift I could've asked for."

Elizabeth let herself cry, and Monroe held her up. She didn't care if anyone was watching. People bustled around her, and the train whistle announced the six thirty was leaving the depot for Cañon City, but it didn't matter. She was home, and her brother was here. When she could cry no more, she backed up and wiped her face with her hands.

"Elizabeth?"

She turned to a voice behind her. It was Hannah. Her veins seemed to go immediately cold. "Is everything all right with Mr. Cooper?"

Hannah smiled. "It's more than all right. He awoke a while ago. He asked for some soup, so I came to fetch you. It took me a bit to find you, but I thought you might wish to bring it to him."

Elizabeth couldn't contain the joy that leapt from her heart. He was awake! He would be fine. "Yes, I will. Right away. Thank you, Hannah!"

As Hannah left, Monroe smiled at his sister. "I'd heard you'd become quite the nurse."

"I don't know about that," Elizabeth said. "But I'm happy to see him awake and well."

"Then go get that soup. We'll talk more later."

She gave him another quick hug before walking as fast as she could to the kitchen. One of the kitchen boys ladled her some chicken soup, and Elizabeth wrapped the bowl in a towel to keep it hot. She was careful not to spill a drop on her way back to Landon. He'd need every bit of this soup to rebuild his energy and remain healthy.

She knocked at the door before entering. "I'm so happy you're awake. I've brought you some—" Elizabeth stopped still in the doorway.

The bed was empty.

Chapter Twenty-four

Landon stood across the street from Murray's Saloon. He'd asked around after arriving in Cañon City just an hour ago. It hadn't taken long at all to discover Redmond's whereabouts. It was nearing midnight—and Christmas Day. Redmond and his other acquaintances from ranches and drives past were in that saloon, likely wondering where he was.

He'd made his way out of the hotel in minutes after he awoke, just in time to board the northbound train. When it arrived, he'd disembarked and walked here. And now he couldn't even bring himself to cross the street.

Instead, he stood in the freezing air amid piles of snow from the blizzard, thinking about how sad it was to spend one's Christmas Eve in a saloon.

What he wouldn't give to be back in the Crest Stone Hotel. He grabbed hold of a nearby post as a wave of heat made him lightheaded. The fever might have broken, but he wasn't fully recovered. In fact, he'd slept most of the train ride to Cañon City. He was weak, and what he really needed was a warm fire and a bowl of hot soup.

Landon backed up a few steps until he could lean against the wall of the hardware store. He still needed to sit, but maybe this would at least let him catch his breath before he made his way across the road. He closed his eyes—just for a moment. Elizabeth's face appeared, and he smiled.

She'd taken care of him while he was ill. Each time he opened his eyes, she was there, checking his forehead, stoking the fire, or simply sitting next to him. Except . . . she didn't want him. She'd said as much while she thought he was sleeping. Just the memory of those words tore through Landon's heart like a knife through skin.

Those were the words that had spurred him to come here. To drag himself out of his sickbed, leave his horse behind, and spend even more of his savings to buy a ticket north to Cañon City. To push himself almost to the door of this saloon on Christmas Eve. To accept the only choice he had.

Landon straightened. The world swayed a little, and he steadied himself with a hand against the wall before moving forward. Yet once he reached the edge of the plank sidewalk, he couldn't step down.

His heart felt as if it were beating inside his head, a drum against his skull, and he thought he might be sick. He pressed a hand against his stomach and tried to steel himself. Luckily, no one was passing on this side of the street so late. He was alone in his misery.

Wheeling backward, he braced himself against the wall again. Why couldn't he seem to move forward? This was his last chance. If he didn't go inside that saloon now and find Redmond, he could forget joining up with them this winter. He could forget finally having enough money for his own place. He'd already spent more than he'd intended at the hotel. He *needed* that money.

And yet he didn't move.

I was so upset with you when you left. Elizabeth's voice again. Landon frowned. He'd run that line—and everything else she'd said while he was "asleep"—through his head over and over, and yet he hadn't really thought about what she meant. He'd put all his attention on the last part, where she more or less said he was a no-good cowboy and that she should've known better than to spend time with him. But that first part . . .What did she mean? Why was she angry with him?

He tried to keep his breathing even as he wiped the sweat from his brow. It wasn't normal to be this hot outside in December. He was still sick. He needed to be in bed. He needed to be back at the hotel.

And he needed to talk to Elizabeth.

Every moment they'd shared those last couple of days before he'd gone out in the snow to rescue the train passengers ran through his mind. He was searching for a clue, something to tell him why she'd felt that way. And then he found one.

It was that moment he'd felt her close off to him. The one that had bothered him all the way to the derailed train, and the one he'd forgotten about as the rescue was underway.

She was angry that he was leaving.

Of course, at that time, he'd planned to ask her to wait for him before he actually left. He hadn't had the time or the privacy to do so before the rescue, and then he'd fallen sick and overheard her, and now he was here.

Landon kicked his boot against the wall. How could he have been so stupid? He was so overcome with his own feelings about her supposed rejection of him when, really, she wasn't rejecting him at all. She was protecting her own heart against what she'd perceived as *his* rejection.

He had to go back to the hotel. Forget the saloon. Forget Redmond. He'd find another way. How, he didn't know, but he knew one thing for absolute certain—he couldn't go on without talking to Elizabeth. It didn't matter now if she disapproved of his original plans, because now *he* disapproved of them. It was ridiculous to think he could spend the rest of his life with her keeping that secret. And what would've happened if he'd gotten caught? He'd been so focused on the money, he'd barely considered that possibility. He'd lost Elizabeth already because of his plans, and he hadn't even gone through with them.

No, he'd go back. He'd tell her everything—including how he felt. If she wanted him, a cowboy who would take years to earn enough for his own spread, then he'd ask her to marry him. And if he wasn't good enough for her, then so be it. At least he'd still have his honor and his integrity. He'd find another way to get what he wanted, somehow.

But first, he had to get back to the hotel.

Chapter Twenty-five

Christmas morning dawned bright and clear. Sarah had already dressed and gone downstairs by the time Elizabeth woke. Elizabeth gazed out the window after she dressed, trying to summon the happiness she knew she should feel on this day. Her friends were getting married, her brother was here, and everyone would be sharing Christmas cheer downstairs. But Elizabeth had to force herself to smile.

Landon was gone.

She shouldn't have been surprised. After all, he'd said he planned to leave. She just hadn't expected it to be so soon. And on Christmas Eve, of all days. He was still sick, and she hadn't even had a chance to speak with him after he woke. He just disappeared, as if speaking with her were the last thing he wanted to do.

She sighed and left the window. It did her no good to stand here, mourning the loss of something she'd never really had. She checked herself one last time in front of the small glass that sat on the dressing table. She'd put on a cheerful face for Penny and Dora, even if she didn't feel cheerful at all inside.

Elizabeth paused at the landing and looked down to the lobby. There weren't many people downstairs yet. She spotted both Penny and Dora in conversation near the tree. Penny gestured at something as Dora shook her head. The image drew a smile to Elizabeth's face. The several feet of snow that now sat outside the hotel had scuttled Penny's plans for outdoor weddings. The ceremonies would now take place in the lobby, and Elizabeth could only imagine what wild idea Penny was proposing to Dora at that moment.

She wrapped her hands around the railing. Her friends had been a comfort to her last night when she'd discovered Landon had left. They'd set aside their wedding preparations to sit with her while she cried—again!—and tried as hard as she could to assure them this was for the best. Of course, she had yet to truly believe that as much as she knew she should.

Landon was an unreliable, selfish cowboy. It was good he was gone. Now she could move on with her new life here as a Gilbert Girl. Perhaps she'd stay here forever and never marry. It wouldn't be such a terrible life, living in this beautiful hotel with so many other women for company.

Although it would be much easier if she hadn't fallen in love with Landon.

She'd realized that late last night, as she lay awake in bed. It had hurt so much because she loved him. The empty feeling in her heart seemed as if it would last a lifetime. But it wouldn't, she knew. It would diminish with time, although she doubted it would ever disappear entirely.

In her heart, she knew this was what she deserved. She'd left her brother with only a hastily scrawled note, and Landon had now left her without a word. She now knew how it felt to be abandoned.

She ran her hands over the railing, willing herself not to cry yet again. It seemed that ever since she'd finally let go with Monroe, the tears were poised to fall again at any moment. It was as if she'd broken a dam inside. When she gathered herself, she descended the stairs. Penny and Dora were so distracted they didn't even notice her as she walked quietly behind them to the tree.

It still stood, tall and beautiful against the frost that covered the lower part of the window. Gifts dangled from the boughs and sat beneath it now, including the ones Elizabeth had purchased for her new friends. They'd all agreed to exchange gifts once the wedding festivities and the luncheon were concluded, but before that night's Christmas dinner.

"Merry Christmas!" Adelaide called from the door of the dining room. She and Sarah joined Elizabeth by the tree.

"Merry Christmas," Elizabeth said in return, even if it felt anything but merry to her.

"Isn't it magnificent?" Sarah said, gazing at the tree. "We never had anything so grand at home."

Elizabeth nodded, grateful for a conversation that had nothing to do with Landon. "My family never had a tree either, although from what I remember, my mother loved to decorate and bake."

"Mother only began having a tree a few years ago," Adelaide said. "She paid a boy to cut one down and drag it through the city. Can you imagine? Dragging trees through the streets of San Francisco?" She laughed. "But it certainly looked beautiful once it was up and all decorated." She smiled wistfully at the tree.

Elizabeth took her hand, happy to think of someone else's feelings besides her own. "Do you miss home?"

"At times. I miss my parents. Sometimes I miss our home and the ease of living in a city." Adelaide grinned at Elizabeth and Sarah. "But I don't miss the gossips. I wouldn't go back. I believe I love it here more."

A smile lifted the corners of Elizabeth's lips. She understood, even though she had no other home to return to. The Crest Stone Hotel had become home, and these girls had become her family.

"How are you?" Penny appeared next to Elizabeth.

"Well enough," she said. Adelaide and Sarah were watching them in curiosity. Maybe Elizabeth would tell them one day. It had been hard keeping the secret, especially from her roommate. But not now, not when the hurt was still fresh. "Are you ready to be married?"

"Am I ever!" Penny said.

The girls laughed. It felt good to laugh, even if Elizabeth didn't feel it all the way to her bones. The weddings were scheduled for eleven o'clock, with the wedding luncheon to follow.

"Then I must see to my pies," Elizabeth said. "I can't leave Mrs. McFarland to bake them all on her own."

Penny gave her a tentative smile. Elizabeth was forcing her cheer, and she could see that Penny knew it. But she'd promised to bake pies for the luncheon, and she wouldn't disappoint her friend, broken heart or not.

Mrs. McFarland was already in the hotel kitchen. They'd considered using the small kitchen in her apartment, but had determined it wouldn't suit for the baking of so many pies. And so Mrs. McFarland had approached Chef Pourrin about using his kitchen. After all, it was her dessert recipes he used most often. He wasn't entirely pleased, but he allowed them the use of one small corner and his ovens. He eyed them now from across the kitchen.

"I don't think he wants us here," Elizabeth said under her breath.

"I believe he thinks our very presence will ruin his dishes," Mrs. McFarland said.

Elizabeth smiled. It felt good to be here with Mrs. McFarland, enjoying quiet companionship while rolling dough and cutting apples. She lost track of time and worry while pressing the edges of the crust and sharing occasional conversation. Hotel staff began to trickle in for their breakfast as the morning progressed.

They'd just placed several pumpkin pies into the ovens when Penny burst into the kitchen.

"Please don't worry. You'll have plenty of pies for your wedding lunch," Elizabeth said as she wiped her hands on a towel.

"I'm not concerned about the pies." Penny waved a hand at the ovens. "Elizabeth, I need your help."

Elizabeth glanced at the crust she'd rolled out for the first apple pie. "Couldn't one of the other girls assist you? We must—"

"No." Penny leveled her gaze at Elizabeth. "It has to be you." She held out a hand and wiggled her fingers impatiently.

"Go on," Mrs. McFarland said with a smile. "The bride is insistent."

"I'll be right back." Elizabeth set the towel down and followed Penny into the dining room. A few of the girls had begun setting up for the large buffet table that would serve various light breakfast foods for the hotel guests. Mrs. Ruby had declared that to be a much better way to celebrate Christmas than the usual service—for both the guests and the Gilbert Girls. And it would help everyone save their appetites for the larger meals to come.

Penny stopped near the doors to the lobby, far enough away from the girls setting up the breakfast table. "Someone is here."

"What do you mean?" Elizabeth didn't expect anyone. She had no one to expect, after all.

Penny pressed her lips together, glanced at the door as if it might be of some help, and then looked back to Elizabeth. "It's Mr. Cooper. He's returned from Cañon City."

Chapter Twenty-six

Landon stood by one of the fireplaces and let the warmth seep into his frozen body. The strain of having stayed awake all night on horseback while still ill made his back ache and his head pound. But none of that mattered. He was at the hotel. Back for Elizabeth.

He glanced toward the closed dining-room doors. It had been some time since Miss May had gone to fetch Elizabeth. The minutes stretched on. Finally warm enough, Landon wandered closer to the doors. What could be happening? His fear grew, and he'd almost convinced himself that Elizabeth had jumped on a horse herself and ridden away when one of the doors finally opened.

Miss May emerged. He searched for Elizabeth over her shoulder, but no one followed her. Clutching the brim of his hat in his hands, Landon waited for Miss May to approach him.

"I'm sorry, she doesn't wish to speak with you." Miss May did look sorry as she spoke.

Even though he'd half expected this to happen, her words were still like a punch to the gut. He took a deep breath. "All right. Perhaps I'll see her at your wedding."

Miss May gave him a slight smile that turned quickly into a frown. "Are you still ill, Mr. Cooper? Perhaps you should lie down."

He shook his head, even as he knew she was right. But if he went to sleep now, he knew he'd sleep through the day. And he refused to give up that easily. "I'll rest in one of those chairs until it's time for the ceremony."

Miss May nodded, but her attention was now elsewhere. "I'm sorry. I must attend to some wedding details." She paused. "Elizabeth was devastated when you left yesterday. But you should speak with her, if you can. She cares for you very deeply."

Landon thanked her before sinking into one of the armchairs that sat before the fireplace. Even though Miss May's words had promised nothing, they gave him hope.

He spent the next few hours trying to force himself to remain awake. He dozed off more than once, and never saw Elizabeth. Either she was hiding upstairs, or she'd passed him while he'd slept.

Close to eleven, a minister—whom Landon recognized as another of the passengers rescued from the train—appeared with a Bible near the tree, and people began gathering in the lobby. Landon forced himself to stand. He could do with solid sleep in a bed, but he wouldn't rest until he'd spoken to Elizabeth. And he knew she wouldn't miss the weddings. He moved through the crowd of people, searching for her.

Just as everyone parted to create an aisle of sorts for the brides to walk, he spotted her. She stood with a group of women, some of whom he recognized as Gilbert Girls. He remained on the opposite side of the aisle, directly across from her. After a moment, she raised her eyes and they landed on him.

He gave her a small smile, but didn't attempt to start a conversation. That would have to wait until after the ceremony. She didn't return the smile, but she didn't look away immediately either. All he needed was a few moments of her time—just long enough to apologize and to tell her the truth, both about how he felt and about why he'd gone to Cañon City.

From somewhere closer to the minister, a violin began playing. A hush fell over the crowd as everyone's attention turned toward the front. Two men stood by the minister—one Landon recognized as a desk clerk at the hotel, the other he'd seen briefly on the derailed train. The latter he remembered hearing was the sheriff of Fremont County, which made him all the more grateful he'd decided not to join Redmond and the others. If their plans hadn't worked out as well as they'd hoped, he could have found himself in this man's jail awaiting a fate he'd never planned on.

The crowd shifted, and Landon turned with them. He caught Elizabeth's eye again as Miss May began her way down the aisle with McFarland on her arm. Elizabeth's gaze shifted to her friend, and a smile finally crossed her face. Her happiness for Miss May—and for Miss Reynolds, who was next down the aisle—made Landon smile too.

Their eyes locked again as they turned toward the front. This time Elizabeth's face softened some. It felt like a victory, even though Landon knew he had a long way to go.

Thankfully, the ceremony was brief. Landon didn't know how much longer he could stand here without anything to hold on to. The minister said the usual words, the two couples made their promises, and Landon felt the strangest yearning to be part of it himself. He snuck another glance at Elizabeth, but her eyes were fixed on her friends and their new husbands. Her angel face was radiant, and despite what she might be thinking about him or her own feelings, she appeared to exude pure happiness for her friends.

That selflessness only made him want her more. He never should have gone to Cañon City, and he'd be angry with himself for the decision for the rest of his life. He'd hurt her in a way she didn't deserve. If Landon had been honest with himself, he'd have admitted the reason he stopped at the hotel to begin with had nothing to do with rest and a warm fire, and everything to do with the fact that he'd never wanted to follow through with his plan. He'd felt cornered by circumstances and had taken what he'd seen as the only way out, despite how he truly felt about it. And now it may have cost him Elizabeth.

He wouldn't let her go without a fight though. The second this ceremony was over, he would speak with her.

If she'd listen.

Chapter Twenty-seven

Elizabeth's eyes kept straying to the handsome yet bedraggled man across the aisle. Landon still looked ill, and about to fall asleep on his feet. The very sight of him made her angry and the happiest she'd ever been all at the same time.

She tried to focus her attention on the wedding ceremony. It was lovely, having it here in the hotel lobby in front of the decorated tree. And both Penny and Dora glowed with joy. Elizabeth was truly happy for her friends who had looked forward to this day for so long, and glancing around, it was clear everyone else felt the same way, even the guests who barely knew them. William, the little boy Landon had rescued, squirmed as his mother watched the proceedings with a smile. Mrs. Ruby, whom Elizabeth would have never thought of as a romantic in any way, dabbed the corners of her eyes with a handkerchief. Mrs. McFarland stood arm-in-arm with her husband, looking as proud as any mother might have. The other Gilbert Girls appeared enraptured with the moment. Adelaide looked especially thrilled for her brother and Penny. And Elizabeth's own brother and his wife, who was still paler than she should be, watched from near the front, his arm around her waist. Seeing her brother so happy lit a candle in Elizabeth's own heart. He deserved all the good in his life.

The joy surrounding her filled Elizabeth with a warmth that seemed to drown her own sadness and confusion as the ceremony went on. And as her gaze wandered to Landon yet again, she wondered if it might be a good idea to allow him to speak with her.

"He keeps looking at you," Sarah whispered from beside her. Her eyebrows raised, and Elizabeth knew she was wondering why.

"I don't wish to speak with him," she said, even though she wasn't entirely certain what she wanted.

That seemed to appease Sarah, though, who nodded and returned her attention to the ceremony. Elizabeth's gaze flitted back to Landon. He was watching her again. It felt as if a string crossed the aisle, connecting him to her. It was maddening, and yet also comforting, and Elizabeth didn't understand it one bit. How could she possibly still feel attracted to a man who'd toyed with her feelings and then left without saying a word?

She bit her lip and turned forward again, although she could still feel those blue eyes on her. The minister pronounced the two couples as man and wife. They kissed to polite applause, and then the violin started up again, this time playing a joyful tune. Both of Elizabeth's friends and their new husbands strode down the aisle as everyone clapped and wished them good luck. Penny reached over to give her a hug as she passed, and Elizabeth grasped Dora's hand and whispered words of congratulations.

Elizabeth wrapped her arms around herself as everyone began to disperse. She should move, and quickly, if she wanted to avoid Landon. Yet she remained fixed in place.

And then there he was, right in front of her.

Next to Elizabeth, Sarah frowned at him. "Come, let's go see Dora and Penny."

Elizabeth closed her eyes a moment, hoping it would give her courage. She opened them again, but he hadn't gone anywhere. He still stood there, right in front of her, those eyes seemingly burning into her soul. That invisible string between them compelled her to remain right here.

"You go," she finally said to Sarah. "I'll be there in a moment."

Sarah paused, as if she wasn't entirely certain Elizabeth meant what she'd said. Finally, she whisked away toward where the newly married couples stood near the tree, receiving congratulations and best wishes.

"May I speak with you?" Landon asked formally as people moved around them, seemingly oblivious to their presence.

"You look as if you might pass out in this lobby," she said.

"Perhaps we should sit?"

Elizabeth hesitated a moment before nodding. He waited for her to take a seat first, which she did, near the tree. The room was so busy, with everyone's attention on the newlyweds, that no one should notice the two of them.

"I was wrong to leave without a word," he said the moment he sat down.

Elizabeth folded her hands in her lap but said nothing.

"You didn't deserve it. I was bullheaded, and I knew if I saw you, I wouldn't go. So I took the coward's way out."

"Then why are you back?"

His jaw worked, and he looked as if the chair was made out of tips of knives. "This work . . . it wasn't for me."

"And you still won't tell me why." Elizabeth began to rise. Sitting here with him was a mistake. "I thought you might be honest with me, but I suppose I was right after all."

He leaned forward and gripped her hand, his eyes on her and his face earnest. "Please sit. I know what you believe me to be. But, angel, I'm not him."

Elizabeth froze. "What did you call me?"

"Angel."

He said it with such tenderness, she thought she might melt. She didn't, of course, but she did sit. His hand remained wrapped around hers. She knew she should pull it away, but she couldn't.

She didn't want to.

I'm not him, he'd said.

Why would he say such a thing, unless . . .

"You overheard me," she said, slowly. He hadn't been asleep when she'd spoken her mind without thinking.

His other hand joined the two that were already entwined. "I did."

Elizabeth wasn't certain if she was relieved or angry. "Why didn't you say anything?"

"I was barely awake," he said. "I tried to speak, but couldn't."

"I see." Her eyes found his. Something was different about them. They were softer somehow, as if he'd tossed away some great burden that had built a wall inside him.

"It was easier for me to believe you didn't want me. It's happened before." He frowned as he spoke. "There was a girl back at one of the ranches where I worked. Aimee. I thought we might be married, but when I asked, she laughed."

The ache in his voice went straight to Elizabeth's heart.

"She said she'd never marry a man like me, a cowboy with nothing to his name."

"I don't see you like that," Elizabeth said. "That was never what concerned me. When I spoke of you being a cowboy, it had nothing to do with money."

Someone laughed loudly from across the room, causing Elizabeth to look up. She half expected to find Mrs. Ruby or Monroe, glaring down at her, but the group in the lobby was still milling about, chatting and completely unaware of Elizabeth and Landon.

"I know that now. Elizabeth, I don't know how your husband treated you, but I need you to know I'm not him." Landon's insistent voice drew her attention back to him.

He was looking at her with the intensity of the sun in summer, and his hands held hers so gently. She wanted to believe him. With all her heart, she wanted just to nod and tell him that yes, she knew he'd be different. But she couldn't, not when experience had taught her otherwise. "Colin was kind to me too, in the beginning. Then he changed. How am I to know you wouldn't do the same?"

"I could tell you I won't," he said. "I could promise you that I'd always treat you as the angel you are. But you'd have to trust me."

"You already left me once," she said quietly. "Why should I trust you after that?"

He took a deep breath and shifted their hands. "I suppose you shouldn't."

Chapter Twenty-eight

Elizabeth's hand went stiff between Landon's. Her beautiful angel eyes widened. "What do you mean?"

Landon drew a deep breath. He had to tell her, no matter what her reaction might be. One thing had become crystal clear as he stood on the freezing street in Cañon City, exhausted but finally thinking straight: he couldn't keep this decision he'd almost made from her. "I wasn't honest with you, not entirely."

"I asked you more than once—"

"I know, and I'm sorry I didn't confide in you. To be honest, Elizabeth, I was ashamed. I feared what you might think of me." He paused, trying to get a read on what might be going through her mind.

"Go on," she said, her voice cautious. But she didn't pull away from him, and that alone gave him courage.

"I've been working on ranches and driving cattle my entire life. As soon as I was old enough, I was working as a ranch hand. I like that work, but it started to wear on me that I was always doing it for other people. I wanted to do it for myself. I want my own place, my own herd."

"I understand that," Elizabeth said. "There's nothing shameful about wanting to have your own land."

It hurt to see that kindness in her eyes. He wondered if she'd look at him the same way once he finished telling her what he'd planned. "I've saved my wages for years. Other men would spend everything they earned after a drive, but I put my money away. It's not enough though, and it won't be for years to come."

Her other hand caressed the back of one of his. It was such a sweet, simple gesture, meant to comfort. He'd reached the hardest part of his story, and pressing on seemed to be the equivalent of going outside right now and riding back to Cañon City.

"There are some men I know, that I worked with on ranches and drives throughout the years. One of them had the idea to spend the winter . . ." He forced himself to look her in the eyes. "To spend the winter rustling the cattle from the ranches where we'd worked."

Her mouth opened just a little before she clamped it shut.

"That's why I went to Cañon City, to meet up with them. It would've been good money, more than I've ever made. But Elizabeth, I couldn't do it."

Her face softened, and just seeing that gave him hope.

"I'd wrestled with it for days. I stopped here as an excuse, and then I couldn't seem to leave, even though I spent more money on a room here than I should have." He laughed dryly. "At first I stayed because I had doubts about the job, but later it became more about . . . you."

She watched him, saying nothing. But her hand moved against his again, and just that one small touch brought a smile to his face. All around them, people talked and laughed, but here, next to the tree, it was as if they were entirely alone.

"I didn't want to leave you. But I had nothing to offer you. I'd nearly made up my mind to take the job and never tell you what I'd done. I wanted to ask you if you'd wait for me. But then I heard what you said while I was sick."

Elizabeth shut her eyes briefly and sighed. "I thought you didn't want me," she said.

Her words pierced his heart. "I'm so sorry, Elizabeth. All I can say is that once I got to town, I realized I couldn't go through with it. I couldn't leave you without telling you how I felt. And if you accepted me, I couldn't lie to you for the rest of our lives. I love you, Elizabeth."

Her lip trembled and her hand stilled.

"Do you trust me?" he asked.

"You've asked me that before." She bit her lip before continuing. "The answer hasn't changed."

"Then believe me when I tell you that will never change. *I* won't change. Whether that's good or not is up to you to decide," he said, hoping she could see the humor in his words.

He got a tiny smile in return, and so he pressed forward. "I will always treat you well. Because I love you, and I would never want to hurt you." Landon raised a hand and ran his fingers down the side of her face, not caring who might see.

Elizabeth closed her eyes at his touch, but she said nothing.

"Please, tell me what's on your mind," he said when he could stand it no longer.

"I'm scared," she said, her eyes wide open now. "I love you, and I'm terrified."

"I understand, but you need not be." He let himself go to one knee on the floor in front of her, ignoring the lightheaded feeling that came with such a quick movement, her hand still clasped in his. "I want to love you for the rest of my life. I want to take care of you, and keep you from ever being afraid again. And I promise to be nothing but honest with you. I don't have much now, but if you can wait, someday we'll have land and a home of our own. Elizabeth, will you marry me?"

She closed her eyes again briefly, and he feared she was about to reject him. But then they opened, and she smiled. "I do trust you. And I love you, Landon. So yes. Yes, I'll marry you."

All exhaustion forgotten, Landon leapt to his feet. He placed a hand on either side of her face and held her there for a moment. He was so lucky that this perfect, wonderful woman had come into his life.

Her eyes searched his face, and a smile played on her lips. "Are you going to kiss me yet?"

He laughed. "As much as I can, angel." And with that, he met her lips. She wrapped her arms around him, and he moved his hands to pull her closer. She melted into him, a real-life angel in the glow of the candles from the tree.

Landon finally forced himself to pull away. He ran his fingers across her forehead, pushing back errant locks of her hair. "Come," he said. "I have an idea."

Her hand in his, he led her across the room to where the minister was speaking with a small group of people.

"Reverend," he said the moment they were close enough for the man to hear him. "I don't suppose you'd perform a third wedding today?"

Chapter Twenty-nine

The wedding lunch was a lovely meal, with everyone in high spirits. Elizabeth tried to enjoy the food and the company, but she found she spent most of the meal with her hand in Landon's, sneaking glances at him and wishing it were evening already so they could be married. As soon as the lunch ended, the girls retreated to the lobby to exchange gifts.

Monroe led Landon away—much to Elizabeth's dismay—to the men's parlor along with Mr. Gilbert and Sheriff Young.

"I didn't think he'd ever let you go," Penny said teasingly as they sat before the tree.

"Oh, please! You and the sheriff haven't let go of each other since the wedding," Emma said.

"Yes, we did! I had to cut my meat, and I needed both hands for that," Penny replied.

Elizabeth laughed along with her friends. Adelaide, impatient to get to the gifts, began handing them out. The girls opened them one at a time, marveling over each gift in an effort to make it last longer. As Dora opened the pretty hair comb Elizabeth had gotten for her—the one Caroline had explained was all the rage back in New York—Elizabeth wrapped her arms around herself and thought about how perfect this Christmas was.

Here she was, in a beautiful hotel with girls who had quickly become her friends, in front of a warm fireplace and a tree she'd helped decorate, waiting on the return of a man she knew would always come back. Last Christmas, she'd sat alone in a tiny one-room house that was no better than a shack, chilled because they'd run out of wood to burn, and wondering if her husband would be home for the meager Christmas meal she'd made. Looking at the happy faces of her friends, and knowing she'd never be lonely again on Christmas or any other day, Elizabeth could hardly believe the difference a year had made. She sent up a quick prayer of thanks before Emma drew her attention back to her surroundings.

"I must tell you all something," she said. "I didn't want to draw attention away from your weddings, but now that we have another wedding this evening …" She paused and smiled at Elizabeth.

"Well, what is it?" Penny said, scooting closer to Emma.

"I—that is, *we*—Monroe and I—are expecting a child."

Elizabeth leapt up and knelt in front of Emma, flinging her arms around her newfound sister in a hug. "I am so happy for you!"

"Oh, I was hoping you would be!" Emma held Elizabeth's hands in her own. "I only hope you and Mr. Cooper will be here to meet the baby."

Elizabeth smiled at her. "I do too, but that isn't something we've discussed yet."

The other girls congratulated Emma, who beamed as brightly as the candles on the tree. Elizabeth sat back and marveled at how happy everyone seemed to be. This truly was the perfect Christmas.

"Now I believe we have another wedding to prepare for," Penny announced, taking Elizabeth by the arm and tugging her gently until she stood.

Penny led Elizabeth to the stairs. An entire crowd of girls followed them, and Elizabeth laughed as at least ten of them found their way into her and Sarah's room. Soon enough, she found herself dressed and her hair fixed in a loose chignon with a sparkling comb Sarah lent her.

Adelaide bent down to pinch some color into Elizabeth's cheeks, and Elizabeth had to swat her away.

"I think Landon will still marry me even if my face is the same color as the snow outside," she said.

"You needed a *little* color," Adelaide protested.

"Oh! I almost forgot." Caroline slid through the group of girls crowded around Elizabeth and held out her hand. "Earbobs!"

Elizabeth peered into her palm at the most beautiful pair of shining pearl earbobs. "Caroline! Those must have cost a fortune!"

"I have another pair. Please, take them. Consider them a gift."

"I couldn't—" But Elizabeth's protest was already lost as Penny reached for one of the pearls. Before Elizabeth knew it, they were affixed to her earlobes.

Penny stepped back, and Elizabeth glanced down at herself. She wore a dark green skirt and bodice that had come from Millie, a necklace from Edie, the earbobs from Caroline, and the comb from Sarah. Tears pricked the corners of her eyes, but Elizabeth refused to cry from happiness, of all things, on her wedding day.

"Thank you all so much," she said, her fingers resting on Edie's necklace.

"You look lovely," Dora said, taking her hand. "And now we must get you downstairs, else your intended will wonder what we've done with you."

The girls escorted Elizabeth to the stairs. As she descended, she couldn't keep the smile from her face. The lobby was especially beautiful in the glow of the evening lamps, crackling fires, and the candles on the tree. People had gathered again, forming an aisle just as they had for Dora and Penny's weddings, but angled toward the tree this time. The minister stood in front of the tree, with Landon at his side.

Elizabeth nearly stopped on the stairs. Landon wore a suit! She hardly thought he'd wear his worn work clothing and scuffed boots to their wedding, but she hadn't expected a suit. She didn't know where it had come from, but it looked as if it had been made to fit him. He smiled at her as she reached the bottom step, and all she wanted to do was to run to him, grab hold of him, and never let him go again.

The girls filtered past her to join the other guests, wishing her luck and hugging her as they passed. Monroe appeared next to her and offered her his arm.

"Congratulations," Elizabeth whispered to him.

He looked puzzled for a moment before grinning at her. "Emma told you?"

"She might have told all of us," Elizabeth said.

"I'm not surprised. She's been wanting to share our secret for a while now." Monroe leaned closer as everyone turned and waited for them to walk down the aisle. "Are you happy, Lizzie?"

Elizabeth bit her lip to keep her own smile from overtaking her entire face. "So very much. I never thought it was possible to be so happy."

"You deserve it," he said, and Elizabeth thought her heart would burst from her chest. All those years of guilt she'd built up over what she'd done to him had melted in an instant.

"Thank you, Monroe. For everything."

"I've already informed your husband-to-be that if he ever says an unkind word to you, he'll be dealing with me." He glanced down the aisle toward where Landon waited, shifting impatiently next to the minister.

The words warmed Elizabeth to her core, even though she knew they were unnecessary. "I appreciate your brotherly concern."

"You're stuck with me now. No more disappearing."

She laughed. "Never again. I promise."

Monroe gave her that crooked smile she remembered from their youth, the one that had always gotten him out of trouble. "Now let's get you married before your groom comes marching down the aisle for you."

So many familiar faces beamed at Elizabeth as Monroe guided her toward Landon and the minister. She couldn't help comparing this wedding to the rushed one she'd had with Colin at the home of a justice of the peace seven years ago.

As Landon took her arm from Monroe, who kissed her cheek before going to join Emma, Elizabeth wondered if maybe her past hadn't happened for a reason. After all, if she hadn't left and endured what she had in California, she never would've needed to seek her brother out here, in this snowy valley, miles and miles from the nearest real town. And she would never have met Landon.

A sense of peace settled over her as she and Landon stood before the minister. They said their vows in front of the tree he'd cut down and she'd decorated with her friends. She couldn't help but think of it as a symbol of their new lives, of the life and the home they'd build together.

The minister pronounced them man and wife, and Landon gently placed his hand on Elizabeth's cheek to draw her in for a kiss. She wanted to drown in it, to never come up for air again, but he finally pulled back and laughed. "I promise you there will be more of that," he whispered.

"I'll hold you to that promise," she replied.

Landon wrapped her hand in his, and they turned to walk back down the aisle.

As she faced her new friends and the hotel guests, Landon's hand warm and protective around her own, all Elizabeth could think was how magical this Christmas was. It had brought her friendship, family, and love. And as she glanced up at her new husband, she knew she would treasure these memories for always.

Epilogue

Christmas dinner was a merry, loud, and filling affair. As soon as Elizabeth took her last bite of Christmas pudding, Landon leaned over to whisper in her ear.

"Come with me." He gave her a devilish grin before taking her hand and leading her around the table and through the dining-room doors into the empty lobby. Everyone was gathered for the Christmas dinner, and not even a desk clerk was posted in his usual place.

"Where are we going?" she asked as they walked quickly past the twinkling tree toward the stairs.

"Run and get your coat," he answered.

"Outside?"

All he did was smile and pull her up the stairs. They parted ways on the second-floor landing. Bewildered, Elizabeth retrieved her coat, hood, and gloves as quickly as possible and raced back to meet Landon downstairs.

It didn't take him long. He moved quickly down the stairs, and she paused for a moment to admire her new husband. *Husband.* If she weren't wearing layers of clothing, Elizabeth would have pinched herself. After everything that had happened, it was almost impossible to believe it was true.

"Are you ready?" he asked.

"I half expected you to lie down and finally sleep," she replied. "You still aren't well." How he'd continued through the day was beyond her, considering how exhausted he'd been when he returned.

"A beautiful woman agreed to marry me, and that's keeping me wide awake." He grabbed hold of the doorknob and opened the door to the dark night.

But it wasn't so dark at all, Elizabeth realized as she let Landon lead her outside. Someone had shoveled all the snow that had fallen in the carriage path that led down to the depot, and the moon above illuminated the brightness of the snow all around them. The stars winked in the sky, like an array of tiny candles that stretched as far as she could see. And in the window, just to their right, the actual candles on the tree beckoned any traveler to come inside to warmth and merriment.

The cold air burned the inside of Elizabeth's nose, but she was warm in Landon's arms. He wrapped them around her and pulled her back close against him.

"Merry Christmas," he whispered in her ear, as if he were afraid to disturb the silence of Christmas night.

Elizabeth turned her head slightly, just enough to see the outline of his jaw. "Merry Christmas. I believe this may be my favorite Christmas."

"You believe?" he said in a joking voice.

Elizabeth smiled. He was so lighthearted now that he'd unburdened himself from the work he'd thought he needed to do this winter. "I suppose I know."

"You suppose? Angel, you offend me."

She laughed, and the sound disappeared into the stillness of the night. "It's so lovely out here. I wish I could see this valley in the spring. I can only imagine how beautiful it is with wildflowers and green leaves on the aspens."

"You may have that opportunity," Landon said.

Puzzled, Elizabeth turned in his arms to face him. "What do you mean?" They hadn't had much opportunity to discuss where they'd go once they left the hotel.

He moved his hands so they settled on her lower back. "Mrs. McFarland found me earlier. She seemed to know I was in need of better work." He paused a moment, as if waiting for her to admit she'd shared this information with Mrs. McFarland.

But Elizabeth shook her head. "I've said nothing to her—or anyone—about that."

"Hmm." Landon looked over her shoulder into the chilly night before returning his gaze to Elizabeth. "She told me her brother owns a ranch not too far north of here. One of his neighbors is getting older and has no children to inherit his land. He's looking for a partner to run the place with him and take it over when he's gone."

Elizabeth gazed up at him. Hope blazed in his eyes as he watched her reaction. She clasped her arms tighter around him. "How did Mrs. McFarland know the perfect man for that opportunity?"

He grinned at her. "I honestly don't know. So should I ask her to send the man a letter? Would you be happy living on a ranch, even if it wasn't fully ours yet?"

"Landon Cooper, this is your greatest dream. If you don't ask Mrs. McFarland to send a letter, I'll saddle up a horse and ride there myself tonight."

Landon threw back his head and laughed. "All we need is you getting sick too." He quieted and brought a hand to her face. "Thank you."

She pressed her cheek into his touch. Light flurries of snow began to fall, and she blinked them away from her eyelashes. "I'm happy anywhere with you, but a ranch that will someday be ours? It sounds perfect." She paused. "Perhaps all of this was meant to be. Perhaps this happened because you chose to leave Cañon City."

Landon said nothing. Instead, he wrapped his hand around the back of her neck and drew her toward him for a kiss, as the snow drifted down around them and the light from the tree in the window illuminated the night.

And all Elizabeth could think was that this would be a Christmas to remember, forever.

THANK YOU FOR READING! I hope you enjoyed Elizabeth and Landon's story! Next, you have to find out what secret Edie is keeping from the rest of the girls, and what happens when she meets Deputy James Wright. You can get their story, *On the Edge of Forever*, here: http://bit.ly/EdgeofForever

To be alerted about new books—and to find out more about the upcoming Crest Stone mail order brides series—sign up here: http://bit.ly/catsnewsletter I give subscribers a free download of *Forbidden Forever*, a Gilbert Girls prequel novella (it tells the story of Mr. and Mrs. McFarland). You'll also get sneak peeks at upcoming books, insights into the writer life, discounts and deals, inspirations, and so much more. I'd love to have *you* join the fun!

Turn the page to see a complete list of the books in the Gilbert Girls series, and all of my other historical western romance books.

More Books by Cat Cahill

Books in *The Gilbert Girls* series
Building Forever[1]
Running From Forever[2]
Wild Forever[3]
Hidden Forever[4]
Forever Christmas[5]
On the Edge of Forever[6]
The Gilbert Girls Book Collection – Books 1-3[7]
***Crest Stone Mail-Order Brides* series**
A Hopeful Bride[8]
A Rancher's Bride[9]
***Brides of Fremont County* series**
Grace[10]
Molly[11]
Other Sweet Historical Western Romances by Cat
***The Proxy Brides* series**

---

1. http://bit.ly/BuildingForeverbook

2. http://bit.ly/RunningForeverBook

3. http://bit.ly/WildForeverBook

4. http://bit.ly/HiddenForeverBook

5. http://bit.ly/ForeverChristmasBook

6. http://bit.ly/EdgeofForever

7. http://bit.ly/GilbertGirlsBox

8. https://bit.ly/HopefulBride

9. http://bit.ly/RanchersBride

10. http://bit.ly/ConfusedColorado

11. https://bit.ly/DejectedDenver

A Bride for Isaac [12]
A Bride for Andrew [13]
A Bride for Weston[14]
***The Blizzard Brides* series**
A Groom for Celia [15]
***The Matchmaker's Ball* series**
Waltzing with Willa[16]

---

12. http://bit.ly/BrideforIsaac

13. https://bit.ly/BrideforAndrew

14. https://bit.ly/BrideforWeston

15. http://bit.ly/GroomforCelia

16. https://bit.ly/WaltzingwithWilla

About the Author, Cat Cahill

A sunset. Snow on the mountains. A roaring river in the spring. A man and a woman who can't fight the love that pulls them together. The danger and uncertainty of life in the Old West. This is what inspires me to write. I hope you find an escape in my books!

I live with my family, my hound dog, and a few cats in Kentucky. When I'm not writing, I'm losing myself in a good book, planning my next travel adventure, doing a puzzle, attempting to garden, or wrangling my kids.

Made in United States
Troutdale, OR
02/17/2024

17766221R00083